Frederick Charles Moncreiff

The X Jewel

A Scottish romance of the days of James VI.

Frederick Charles Moncreiff

The X Jewel
A Scottish romance of the days of James VI.

ISBN/EAN: 9783337019822

Printed in Europe, USA, Canada, Australia, Japan

Cover: Foto ©Andreas Hilbeck / pixelio.de

More available books at **www.hansebooks.com**

A SCOTTISH ROMANCE OF THE DAYS OF JAMES VI.

BY THE

HON. FREDERICK MONCREIFF

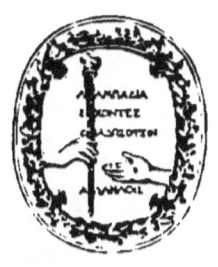

NEW YORK

HARPER & BROTHERS PUBLISHERS

1896

THE X JEWEL

CHAPTER I

I was brought out of the Low Countries into Scotland in the year 1585—by whom I need not to say here. For though it is now more than twenty years since the things I speak of passed, and they are forgotten by some who might have remembered them, there are others still in life who remember but may not wish them to be stirred. This, however, can I say: that my coming back was known to one who required it, and whose wish it was scarce possible for me to pass by.

So, on the 3d of May in the above year, having made a quick passage from the Scheldt on a quiet sea, I landed at the Fastcastle, near to Eyemouth, at eight hours of the morning. And glad indeed was I that morning when I jumped on to the jetty and ran up the steps leading to

1

the keep, which, as many know, are cut from the rock, and not easy to be found.

I was glad—what else should I be? I had the yearning for my native land which is common to my race, and I had no great heart to remain in the service I had kept for the greater part of ten years. Monsieur was gone; the Poor Frog of the Queen of England was dead of a fever. The Prince of Orange was dead by the bullet of Balthasar Gérard, a mean fanatic and hired assassin. For this Prince lived at a time not yet distant when money and patents of nobility were given for the doing of murder. The Pope, for whom my Pastors have many injurious words, naming him Antichrist and that Man of Sin, offered his rewards openly—even as he might send the crier about for a lost dog. But when the English Harry, or the Queen his daughter, had a mind to the removal of a troublesome person, they handled the matter with some decency through the medium of an ambassador or envoy, though they paid not as handsomely as the Pope.

When the Prince fell the life of the cause in the States seemed to die, and to none was this so much due as to the termagant who misgoverned England. Surely there was scarce an evil thing done either in the Low Countries or my native Scotland which she had not labored to bring about. Her ambassadors came to Edinburgh with instructions to make it impossible to govern the country, to set one interest against another, and to lie to all—to King, Council, Ministers, Nobility, and Barons. Nobody should know this better than I; but, if the commonty had known the truth, I fairly believe that they would have flayed the English ambassador alive in the Grassmarket and sent his skin to his mistress. This and much more might they have done at that time with impunity; for if the Queen of England feared nothing else, she did fear a war with the Scots.

I left a service which had been kind to me, and I had heard from those who had the best reasons for knowing that I was returning to a land "where nane was in account but he that could either kill or reve his neighbor." Well, I could kill and reve with the best of them—in a good cause, be it said. It was my trade.

In the keen morning air I ran quickly up the steps leading from the jetty, so that I was forced to stay for breath before I had compassed half of the distance—in faith, an evil place. The cliffs, which are very high on this coast, go down almost sheer into the sea. At one part, where a point juts out into the North Sea, there is a platform half-way down the cliff, which is reached from the jetty below by a flight of steps cut out of the rock. On this platform stands Fastcastle, and half-way up the steps to it on this May morning stood I, panting for breath and looking down upon the many-colored sea.

As I stood, my head swimming somewhat with the exertion of running after being cramped in the boat, the voice as of one singing came up to me out of the sea. It came dimly, as from a great distance; if so I may say, it struggled to me; but the words were not the less plain to be heard, and what I heard and remember was somewhat to the following purpose:

"Five fathom deep,
Beneath the keep,
Not forgotten, not forgiving;
Better to be loose and living
Upon the sea
Than bide with me."

Now it may be that I was in some measure oppressed by the weird aspect of the place. But there is no Scotsman who does not know the meaning of "loose and living" as well as he knows the name of Douglas. So it came to pass that I, who have never rejected these messages of God, went down the steps more quickly than I came up and stopped the disembarkation of my baggage, resolved that on no consideration would I land at the Fastcastle.

I had no sooner done this than one came down from the castle whom I believed to be the Laird of Lundygrange, the keeper or owner of the place; but as I never saw him before or afterwards, I cannot speak of this with certainty. I had reason to believe that this man would both allow me to land and assist me with horses for my journey to Edinburgh, but now I was no longer willing to trust him.

"I believe I have the pleasure to welcome to my poor castle the Colonel Andrew Eviot," said he, saluting me with much courtesy.

"Excuse me, Laird," I replied; "I am but simple Capitaine, and great as is the pleasure of seeing you and your hospitable castle, I am sorry my business requires that I should push on to Edinburgh without delay. Indeed, I trust you will furnish me with horses to transport myself and my servants."

"Impossible; quite impossible. Horses are at the moment the most expensive and most valuable possession a man can have in Scotland. They are hardly come by, and I have not enough for my own service. You had better stay a few days with me and look about you—the coast is very fine and the air bracing."

"Nay," said I, after thanking him profusely for his offer of hospitality, "if I may not ride, I must walk;" and I looked resolute, for I would compel him to show his hand. Whereupon he gazed somewhat sadly and sympathetically at me, and said:

"You had better stay: believe me, sir, the air of Edinburgh may not be good for you just now."

"Good or bad, I'm going to test it."

"Nay, nay," he returned, irritably, "it is the King's opinion, not mine." He spoke as one who had been reluctantly compelled to tell a disagreeable fact, but I felt that I held him committed.

"If so the King wishes it to be, you doubtless have his warrant, and I shall crave a sight of it."

"I have what is as good—the Chancellor's letter, in which he says that he holds the King's commission."

"The Chancellor, forsooth!" cried I. "Captain James? You may tell Captain James that I obey the King first, and after him I may think of obeying the Chancellor."

At this my man's eyes opened very wide, as if he had been listening to some astounding blasphemy and could not believe his ears. Now my experience had taught me that in interviews which may end in "inconvenients," a man should cast his eyes about betimes, and know what he is going to do when the rub comes. In this case I saw very clearly what I had to do. Going close up to the Laird, so close that by putting forth his hand he could touch me and no more, I looked earnestly in his eyes.

"Friend Lundygrange," said I, "ye are but a poor bungler, and were I not in a hurry I should pull the lugs off your head. It is not for such as ye to meddle with things of Estate. They are ticklish enough for those whom God has furnished with brains to their heads, but they will grind the Laird of Lundygrange and his like to powder. Ye mislike that I call ye bungler. What are ye, then, that having yon message for me kept it not until I was within your walls? Whereas now, look ye, I shall simply go aboard again, and, bidding adieu to this inhospitable place, commend ye to the mercies of Captain James."

Thereupon it fell out as I thought. Being a stout man, and seeing me within his grasp, the Laird reached forth his hand to seize me by the neck of the corselet. When his hand was about an inch from my neck, I struck him a blow with my gauntleted hand on the chest, which placed him upon a heap of mackerel lying some paces in his rear. God made my arms longer than they ought by rights to be. But the keeper of Fastcastle knew not that, nor that in the States I was surnamed the iron-armed, else the result might have been different.

As it was, the few men who had followed him down from the keep were lightly armed, and as they received no orders from their master, who was for the moment unable to give any, they concerned themselves in picking him out of the dirt. In the meantime I went on board unmolested, and had no difficulty in persuading my skipper to land me at Berwick.

This change of plan was somewhat embarrassing, because the English were chary of passing anybody into Scotland. There were in London, Newcastle, and Berwick banished Lords and banished Ministers, and many other banished Scots who were neither Ministers nor Lords. And the Amity between the Courts of London and Edinburgh required that the English authorities should give no open countenance to those who passed backward and forward between the exiles and their friends in Scotland.

Moreover, in order to reach Berwick, we had to pass Alexander Home of Manderston, who watched for little ships as a spider watches for flies, and but lately had taken a boat belonging to the Earl of Angus coming from Tantallon to

Berwick. Nevertheless did we clear out from the Fastcastle amid great noise from the fowls upon the crag and with a bow to the keeper of the place. Then turning our backs to the Law of North Berwick and the Bass Rock—it was a clear morning, and I saw both very plainly—we made for Berwick. There I found those who had interest enough to pass me unnoticed through the English posts, and to furnish me so effectually with what I required that early next morning, accompanied by David Carryg and another named John Sloan, I rode past the tennis-court to the north of Holyroodhouse, and into Edinburgh by the Watergate, marking the time on the horologe in the King's Garden to be six hours. And so, once more, after long years, was I within thy walls, O most beautiful and most filthy of cities! where the butchers hang out upon the street the hides of the meat they have killed, where the kennel runs with the garbage of vegetables and all manner of refuse, and the blood of last night's brawl lies damp upon the causeway. Yet, for all thy dirty face, I would not have been elsewhere; and so hungry was I that I could almost have eaten the landlord of Robertson's Inns.

CHAPTER II

I CARED little for the scuffle on the pier-head at the Fastcastle, but the reception I met with in Edinburgh fairly took me aback. I came home in the belief that—it might be quietly and not officially—some honorable service would be required of me, and before I had been three hours in Edinburgh I was served with a peremptory notice to appear before the Council at eleven o'clock.

I had dressed myself with care, purposing to seek out the lodging of the Colonel Stewart, whom his Highness greatly affected at this time, so that the messenger of the Council had the benefit of my brigandine jacket with its facings of velvet and silk, which was lined in the inside with steel scales. He beheld, moreover, my hose, which lay loose round the hips, and fitting tight to the knees, were tied below with bows. His notice, however, caused me at once to forget these little vanities, for I marvelled at it not a little. But when the messenger had gone, my host, who was better acquainted with his office than I was, inquired in a whisper whether I was for Antichrist or Mr. Andrew Melvill.

"Saunders," says I, "why think you that the Council would only stretch forth its hand against the followers of these two?"

"I think so because there is nothing so perilous as religion. Eh! man—may God forgic me!—but I could drive a grand trade in this sinful auld toun if it werena for religion. It's swarming wi' men wi' maisters, and—what's waur—men wanting maisters; but a body canna get peace to entertain them."

"What do you mean, man?"

"Weel, sir, I'm speaking not of my own religious opeenions, which are sound enough, but of those of other folk. There are plenty of loons in this toun with faces long enough to turn a cup of ale sour, who would put the Bailie of the ward on to me for harboring you—always supposing you were a Papist. And although the Bailie hath prosecuted no man these ten years—as ye can see by the state of the causeway—he would have to move against me. I would maybe be finit, or deprivit of my license to import wines from Bordeaux or Oporto. Or if they were mindit to carry things with a high hand, I might be cast into the Thieves' Hole for a twalmonth, and booted before I would win out."

"Aye; and if I were for Mr. Andrew?"

To my surprise Saunders made no reply to
this, but looked moodily on the ground, as if he
had heard not. On my repeating the question
he tried out of courtesy to his guest to smile, but
it was a wan, foolish, sickly smile, and he looked
again upon the ground. At last he said, with
some earnestness: "Ye'd maybe not notice that
ye're summoned for eleven o'clock, whereas it's
weel kenned that the Council rises at eleven,
and does not sit again till two in the afternoon.
Now if ye are a friend of Mr. Andrew's I would
beseech ye to have your horses saddled at once
and brought to the foot of my garden. Ye could
go by the Back of the Canongate, through the
Kirk-of-Field Port, to the fields, and a few hours'
ride would bring ye to the wild Earl of Bothwell's country."

"No, Saunders, I shall bide my chance. I
mean not to cut or burn for either Mr. Andrew
or Archbishop Adamson."

"It's easy seen," grumbled Saunders, "that
ye ken naething about this country that speir at
me that gate, and flee at my nose when I answer
ye. Dinna ye ken that the Earl of Arran, him
that was Captain James Stewart, holds the sway
down yonder?" (Here he waved his hand com-
prehensively towards the east.) "There is nane

to say Nay to him if it be not his brother, the Colonel. They say the Colonel is very inward with his Highness. It seems but yesterday that the Earl made his peace with the Kirk and went regularly to the sermon, very humble in appearance and devout. There was to be an end of the feud between the Kirk and the Council, but it a' ended in smoke. One fine morning it was fund that the Ministers — them as were unco guid, or, as ye might term them, Puritans—had gone south on very urgent business, and to this day they are going to and fro upon the face of England seeking rest for the soles of their feet."

This was not news to me. The King, who was but a lad eighteen years of age, was said to be ruled by the Earl of Arran. This so-called Earl, by name James Stewart, was a younger son of his house, who, having spent some time as a soldier of fortune in Sweden and the Low Countries, came home and rose into great favor with the King. By some fantastic claim he dispossessed the Hamiltons of the earldom of Arran, and gathered to himself I know not what offices of trust and value. If my memory fails me not, he was at this time High Chancellor, Governor of Edinburgh and Stirling Castles, Provost of Edinburgh, Captain of the Guard, President of the Council, and Lieutenant-general of Scotland.

Such distinctions are not in my country gathered by a mushroom nobleman without interfering with other folk; so it came about that there were sundry factions eating out their hearts in England and waiting for a chance to end the sway, or the life, of Captain James—that is to say, the factions of the Hamiltons and Douglases, the Ruthven Lords, as they were called, and the Presbyterian Ministers, who styled themselves sometimes the Kirk and sometimes the Saints of God. These, packing up their feuds, made a combination so strong that the Earl of Arran was constrained to pray for the help of the Queen of England or the King of France. But none could say from which quarter the help might come; and inasmuch as one of those monarchs was a Roman and the other of the Reformed Religion the choice of Popery or Presbytery seemed for the moment to hang upon a throw of the dice.

Now the Earl had, as I have said, a brother who was known to all Scotland as the Colonel or Coronall. Some called him the Crownal. And I, having dressed myself with great care, was about to go in search of the lodging of this same Colonel when Saunders Robertson interrupted me. I knew him for a true Scot and a good soldier, and I doubted not that for old acquaintance he would find for me at least a formal introduction to the Court. But he knew not why I had come into Scotland, nor did I design to tell him; and that for two reasons. The Colonel had taken to affairs of State, and it behooved him to " run a course," as they say, which might be his brother's, and would probably not be mine. In the second place, I had not much to tell, for I had trusted rather to the weight of those who sought me than to the information they gave. In short, it was thought that, if it were known at whose motion I came, the purpose of my coming would be defeated; and as to that purpose, I should be the less embarrassed in concealing it if it were not intrusted to me until my arrival. My instructions, therefore, were to seek an independent entry to the Court, and await the occasion of my friends.

And now, as it seemed, I was to be introduced to the Court in a character I had scarce looked for. So, perceiving that I had been taken seriously in suspicion by some, I exchanged the brigandine jacket I was wearing for a stout steel corselet, and sallied forth with my two rascals at my heels.

I left these latter in the western court of Holyroodhouse, and gave up my sword to the officer of the guard—for such was the custom at this dangerous moment. I was then carried to the southeastern corner of the second court, and caused to ascend a turnpike stair which led from this point to the first floor. Thence I traversed a passage of some length, and, going through an apartment in which certain idle persons were lounging about, I was brought into a chamber, the windows of which gave both to the north and south.

In this chamber there were five or six persons. One sat at a table writing, while another stood beside him looking over his shoulder. A third, a younger man, walked or lounged about the room, and the rest—one of whom I recognized for Colonel Stewart — stood about the fireplace. All wore the dress then in vogue at the Court of King James, the hose being deeply padded across the loins and hips. There was an absence of bright colors, and these men clearly wore their dress—which was rich enough—for use and not for show; that of him who perambulated the room bore the signs of wear. Indeed, I might at first have taken this man for a Court servitor, but there was something which forbade that.

Nobody spoke, nobody looked up when we entered; not the slightest notice was taken of us.

"Sir," said I, after some small space, to the Groom of the Chamber, who stood beside me, "I was summoned to appear before the Council. This is not the Council-chamber. Are these gentlemen of the Council? This is not well, sir."

"Silence!" he whispered, "the King has desired to see you himself."

"By all means the King; take me to the King. The King, sir—I would see the King." I suppose I spoke loudly, for a deep, measured voice from behind answered:

"Hauld your tongue, ye blethering bull. It becomes ye not to make so free with yon name in our presence. Pericles" (he continued to the man who was writing at the table), "who is the chiel? Who the deil is he?"

"It is Captain Eviot, sir, who was summoned before the Council for returning home without the permission of your Highness and the Council."

"Never mind the Council," replied the young man, collapsing into the arm-chair at the head of the table; "give me the notice."

Having obtained the notice and glanced through it, he tore it into fragments, which he flung into a box provided for rejected supplications and the like idle and unprofitable literature. Then placing his elbows on the table, he leaned his chin on his hands, and with large, dull, lacklustre eyes looked straight into my face. Whereupon I made a low obeisance to him, for by this time I saw he was the King; but he continued to stare moodily at me. I had begun to grow weary and almost to forget his presence, when he said, abruptly :

" What made ye come home, Andrew ?"

I looked in vain for a twinkle in his eye or signal of secret intelligence. This young old man was master of himself as well as of many other persons.

" Sir," I said, " I had served ten years in foreign lands, and I was wearying to see my native Prince and my native country."

" That is weel said, and I am fain to hear it said in the vulgar tongue. But this zeal for your native Prince must be something mature by this time, for it is now six sorrowful years since we took upon us the burden of this realm. Why did ye not ask our leave to return ?"

" I had come sooner, sir, but I might not run from my colors. As for my coming back, I had license to go abroad for ten years, and I knew not that, by the law of Scotland, I required any license to return."

" Aye; are ye there with your law ? As ye appeal unto Cæsar, maybe Cæsar—being for the time our Lord Justice-Clerk — will answer ye. What say you, Cæsar ?"

" Your Highness will remember," said he who stood by the table, "that some stringent order was taken in view of the prevalence of the Pest."

"The Pest, to be sure!" cried the King, fidgeting in his chair; "maybe he has it on him. Speak, man; are ye clengit, purgit of the infection? Know ye not that all men are dischargit from approaching our person at this time without sufficient testimonial of health?"

"I have such testimonial from the burgomaster of Ghent, and I am here by the order of your Highness's Council.

Upon this he who sat writing at the table broke in, saying that the Council had been constrained to pass stringent orders on account of the return of expatriated Scotsmen, especially of Scottish Archers of the Guard, to Fastcastle, and of the many plots and attempts made of late upon the lives of illustrious persons.

"Small need to remind us of that," said the King, as he wriggled out of his chair, and fell to walking about the room, talking—as it seemed—as much to himself as anybody else. "Twa Regents violently and treasonably slain in this country, not to speak of our own father murdered in his bed, within sight of this our palace. Then it was but the other day that William the

Silent, as they called him — he's silent enough now, poor man! — had three drops of lead put through him by a common messenger fellow with a Bible under his oxter.

" Ye can judge, Captain Andrew, what manner of times we live in here when we behoove to wear a bolster like this " (here he indicated the puffed padding of his hose) "about our royal loins, all to escape six inches of cruel steel in the wame. Yet we think not that there are any of Scottish blood who would lay hands, with bloody mind, upon our person—except—it might be—"

"Mr. Andrew Melvill," said the person who was writing at the table; the others, who were now standing by the King's chair, smiled as men scarce daring to laugh.

"Aye," resumed the King; "Mr. Andrew would like to do it, but his religion will not let him. So there is one article of religion upon which he and I agree. But as to the orders of Council, they are mair for the protection of the latent monarchs among you, my Lords, than for ourselves—for I ken that there are *Jacobi Septimi* among ye. Weel, as it is your affair, what say ye I should make of this *Capitanus Redux?*"

The man at the table said "Blackness"; the Justice-Clerk suggested Stirling; a third, whom I afterwards knew to be Lord Rothes, said that the *Arx Episcopi* at St. Andrews was the only safe place for a man not purged of treason or the Pest. There was some laughter at this, in which the King joined not, though I know not why. The Colonel said nothing.

"Na, na," said the King, shaking his head; "it is weel kenned that, for a man of mean substance, confinement in one of our fortresses means ruin; and if we were to dispose him upon the Archbishop, he would hardly escape from St. Andrews with the skin upon his back. Captain Andrew," he added, addressing me, "we like not this peremptory return of yours, this entering at both our front and back doors without so much as crying *Here I am;* it partaketh too much of the appearance of force. It is therefore our wish that, until we are further informed of the occasion of your return to this realm, you retire yourself benorth the Forth within twenty-four hours. You will reside at the Castle of Ruthven, in Strathearn, with which we are weel, we might say ower weel, acquaint; and there you will be entertained by our Chancellor, the Earl of Arran, into whose hands the castle has been rendered for the moment. You will not be restrained in respect of your liberty, except that you will not pass two nights in succession away from your place of ward."

I confess this sentence crushed me for the moment, and I walked back to my lodging scarce conscious of the passers-by. Neglect I had looked for, and even hostility in certain quarters; but to be coldly ignored and packed off like a vagabond beadsman by the man whose name had been used to draw me home—was not this overmuch? I, who had lived a life of action and excitement, to rot and rust in a country tower in the company of husbandmen and occasional jackmen! For a moment I regretted that I had not spoken out plainly, both as to my return to Scotland and the incident at Fastcastle; but on reflection I saw that it would have been folly to do otherwise than I did. Perhaps there was a meaning in it which I could not see, and if I sulked I might miss my chance, if it came. So I struggled to possess myself, and to watch and wait.

I was followed to my lodging by the Colonel, who shook me warmly by the hand, and told me not to be cast down by the inhospitable reception I had met with. He took me into the garden at the back of the lodging, and spoke to me with much earnestness; but I was on my guard with him. His visit surprised me, for I knew it was unusual for a courtier to show kindness or cordiality to one who had, even in a trifling matter, offended the Court. And this was the second thing which made me think that my presence was understood by somebody, and that it was thought worthy of attention.

"Captain Andrew," said he, "I came to you because you are a stranger to the ways of this Court. Here is a copy of the order in your case, signed by the King. The country is in a disturbed state, and furious searches are being made for men, especially in Fife and Strathearn. You may find it convenient to have that about you. Then you will be wise to leave Edinburgh at once. You need not attempt to go by Stirling, for my good brother James has closed the Brig. The Queensferry is a little too near to Kinneil for you; and, besides, on account of the Plague, the ferry-boats are everywhere forbidden to cross, except those plying between Leith and Kingorn."

"You seem," said I, "to think that my Lord of Arran has some grudge against me. That can scarce be, for I have never crossed his path."

"If there is anything," replied he, with some evasion, "which you can tell me in confidence about your return to Scotland, I might be of some real service to you. I stand well with his Highness, and should stand better still but for James. James is my brother, but he is a rascal, and his wife is—well, he will pinch you between his finger and thumb—so—like a fly, for a mere suspicion. But he will first try to win you, and if he fails in that look to yourself. I should be sorry to see you side with him. His motto is, 'Scotland for Captain James Stewart, and after him the devil.' I am for Scotland for the Scots, and in particular for Colonel William Stewart. James has not treated me fairly. His last exploit was to deprive me of the wardship of George Uchiltrie's lass, which the King had promised me; but we have not seen the end of that yet. Now, Eviot, I will travel for you with his Highness, if you wish it; and if you should ever be in a position to assist me, I shall look with assurance for your help."

All this was said with so simple and kindly an air that I would gladly have taken this valiant gentleman into my confidence. But that was not in the game, and I was not the man to turn my cloak. Moreover, he spoke so meaningly that I failed not to see that he invited an explanation. Why? There was something behind this to which I could not as yet reach. So I thanked him warmly for his kindness, and told him that I was always at his service; but that in terms so general that he went not away content.

CHAPTER III

AT this time the common passages across the Forth were, with one exception, forbidden, the Plague of Pestilence having appeared in Fife, being brought, as was said, by a collier to the Wester Wemyss. I therefore crossed by the ship Jonas of Leith to Pettycur, a small haven beside the town of Kingorn. Two Englishmen, most merry fellows, rode thence with me as far as Kinross. But afterwards I had reason to think that they rode rather for their own edification than mine, for I learned that they had haunted Kingorn for some time, and were believed to be in the pay of Mr. Edward Wotton, then the Queen of England's Ambassador in Scotland.

A man of my Lord of Arran's also came with me, on the pretext of showing me the way, but, as I thought, that he might spy upon me; for both then and after I had much ado to escape his presence. I resented this attention all the more because of his countenance, which made men almost doubt the kindness of Almighty

God. His features were naturally so villanous and mean that no one born with the like might either be, or pass for, an honest man. His hair was of the rusty red ascribed to Iscariot, and therefore I would fain have called him Judas. Among his fellows he was Red Rynian, or Rusty Rynian; and as he came from the Debatable Ground, he may have been one of Dick the Devil's bairns. But I was content to call him Barabbas; and although he did once observe that his name was Rynian, he dropped the subject when I told him of my preference.

We were stopped on Kinross Moor by a party of twenty lances belonging to the Earl of Crawford, but not detained. At Kinross were many great wagons carrying timber, slates, and lime to the King's palace at Falkland; the wagoners but little content, although the King had promised, *in verbo Principis*, to be grateful for their service. We saw also many sturdy beggars, idle persons, sickly bodies, and of those who will not work. So by way of Millsforth we passed into Strathearn, crossing the water of Earn by the Brig of that name, and not long after making the Castle of Ruthven.

This place is at no great distance from St. Johnston. The water of Almond running here through a flat basin, a spur or knowe juts out into the flat from the ridge to the south of the water, and on that knowe stands the Castle of Ruthven within a wall, marvellously secure.

It consisted then of two blocks, besides a number of out-buildings. The eastern, and doubtless most ancient, part was a square or oblong keep of four storys, which communicated by means of a turnpike, or newel, staircase, in the northwestern corner of the building. On the upper part of this tower was the apartment assigned to me. The western wing was a later and entirely distinct building, standing at some paces distance from the old keep, and was occupied by persons concerned with the management of the estate. The late Earl of Gowrie having been executed for treason in 1583, his Countess and children were compelled to surrender the whole of his possessions—and among other things this Castle of Ruthven, which for the time was placed in the Earl of Arran's hands.

I had been a fortnight or so in this dreary place when I made a discovery I might have made much sooner if I had cared to be inquisitive. But as I suspected that some manner of watch would be kept on me, I took care that no curiosity should be shown by my men or myself, and spent most of the time in hunting and hawking at a distance from the house. The monoto-

ny of this life began to pall on me, and I took
to remaining more about the castle, having it in
my mind to ride to Falkland and make a per-
sonal appeal to the King, if I could but win a
reservation of his ear.

It happened about this time that a snatch of a
song I had heard, I know not where, began—as
men say—to run in my head. There was a
cursed catch in it. Although I tried to drive it
from me, it met me at every corner: it caught
me on the hills; it wakened me in the morning; it was the last thing I knew before I
slept.

I cudgelled my brain in order to call to mind
where I had heard it, but to no purpose. Some
of the words came back to me, and at times I
found myself singing it.

One afternoon, as the sun was cooling towards the horizon, I had gone to my room, which,
as I have said, was on the top of the eastern
keep. There was a door or window in the room
opening on to the parapet, and facing towards
the subsidiary or western part of the castle. As
I was looking over my wardrobe, I fell into this
song which, though plaintive and catching, I
had begun to curse in silence and aloud. "Ten
fathom deep," I sang; for a bar or two I had
not the words; then the end came thus—

> "Better to be loose and living
> Upon the sea
> Than bide with me"—

whereupon, to my great astonishment, the last two bars were returned to me by a woman's voice from the western block of the castle, with this difference, that the words ran thus:

> "Upon the sea
> Alone with me."

I ran out at once to the parapet; but although I lingered on the spot for a long time to find some sign of the songstress, I had no success. I heard nothing and saw nothing, and I spent the night in cursing my folly for not divining that I had in all possibility been sent to this castle with a purpose.

I was up betimes the following morning, and, resolved to provide myself first with a bird's-eye view of the country and the neighboring buildings, I climbed on to the roof of the keep, concealing myself as well as I could behind the projection of the window, so as not to attract the attention of any one in the fields. I saw but little for my pains that I had not seen before. One thing, however, I did notice. To the south and west of the castle lay a garden or pleasure-ground which was compassed by a high wall. There were two doors in the wall, but these were kept locked, because—as I was told—the garden was reserved for the ground steward, who lodged in the west wing, and he gained access to it by means of a flight of steps from the first floor. The matter had not interested me, but now for the first time I could look into a part of the garden I had not seen before. To the sight there was nobody in it ; but the sun was still low in the sky, and from time to time a long shadow wavered across the far wall.

And I watched not this shadow in vain, for ere many minutes had passed the shadow was followed into view by the substance. As God shall judge me, a lady in the Castle of Ruthven! Young and tall, with a beaver hat and a feather to it, walking to and fro with as much pride as if the place belonged to her, and carrying in the one hand a French book, and in the other a fan and a pair of embroidered gloves. And a strange pleasure she seemed to find in her black satin gown with its silver lace laid over.

"Now, Andrew, or never," I said to myself, hurrying as fast as I could with decency down the turnpike stair. I contrived to reach the back of the garden without being observed, where I found that the wall was not to be scaled without difficulty; but by cutting out the mortar with my dagger, and using a fallen branch to mount with, I scrambled on to the top, and flung myself hastily on to the grass within. As it chanced, the girl was but a pace or two from the spot where I fell, and I looked that this violent arrival of an armed stranger—for the fall was full twelve feet—would scare her. I feared she might cry out, or run towards the house. But she simply glanced at me—contemptuously, I thought — stooping as if to rescue her dress from some imaginary mud or obstruction on the path, and, almost before I recovered my balance, said :

" Well, sir, you have come at last ; you have been a long time about it."

" Come at last !" I gasped, with astonishment ; "and pray, mistress, why should I come at all?"

" Because I am here, sir !" she retorted, tapping the ground with her foot. Here, thought I, is an original who will forgive the fashion of my introduction, but she will be all the more difficult for that. Those strongly marked black eyebrows, and the quick eyes, which had the look of being fully as black, belonged to no sickly girl in her nonage.

" Young lady, what you say is beyond dispute ; but how knew you I would come ?"

" Because I am here, sir ! How often would

you have me say it? Did you think I did not
see you sitting, as you were glued to the roof of
the keep, and gazing abroad like a moon-calf?
Did you expect me to call out to you, 'My pretty
man, Jean Uchiltrie is waiting for you in the
Beech Walk'?"

"Nay; I know not how you could see me.
My eyes are sharp, yet could I not see you."

"If your eyes had not been as dull as your
wits you would have seen a musket-hole in the
wall facing you, and you would have known that
I saw you through that."

"I could not think that weapons so deadly as
Jean Uchiltrie's eyes were levelled on me through
a common musket-hole. But Jean Uchiltrie will
confess that I kept her waiting at most but half
an hour."

"Half an hour too much, if it were half an
hour; but it happens to be a fortnight and four
days."

"Indeed," I protested, "I came hither many
long days ago; but it is one brief half-hour since
I saw you."

"What!" she exclaimed; "is it possible that
you are not the noble captain who fell in love
with me at sight in Edinburgh, and when he
heard that I had gone swore he would dash his
brains out or be after me? No! Nor the Con-

stable of Dundee's son, who left a wife and six children, so they told me, in Stirling, to ride after me along the King's Road to Dunblane?"

"Nor am I he," I said, ruefully, although I suspected that this outburst was meant to cover the disappointment of some other hope my presence had raised. "I saw you for the first time a few minutes ago; but, having seen, I would follow you, not from Edinburgh—which is no great distance—but from the bounds of the earth."

"Get you gone, sir; to the bounds of the earth, if you will. I see that I misknew you. I suppose you are simply one of my jailers, though if you are I cannot think why you should scramble over the wall and fall at my feet like a sack of pease instead of coming in by the door.

"No?" she continued; "well, I am marvellous sorry. You are" (turning round and pretending to look at me critically) "not amiss. Your cloak might have been made at Paris. Ah! it was? Then you look strong—and I am for men who can beat each other to pieces with broadswords. That's a man's sport. I care not for that narrow blade you carry; to fight with the point of a needle is a game for women. Yes; I'm sorry you are not to be my jailer, for you are a bit of

3

a fool, and would have amused me, I dare say, for a fortnight or so."

I say not this did not stir me, for no man—be he as old as Methuselah and as ugly as sin—likes to be despitefully entreated by a young and comely woman. Tarry a space, my young lady, said I to myself, and I will see whether I cannot make you dance to another tune; but to her I said :

"Mistress Jean, you do both me and my sword wrong, as you may find in time. I am no jailer, but a prisoner in this castle, even as you seem to be. I confess I came to your garden because, as you would have it, you were here. And I came over the wall like a sack of meal because I would have heard from you whether I could serve you in aught, whereas I should not have gained entrance by the house."

"How should I know that?" Then, in that tone of mocking levity which I found this strange girl to adopt when she was most serious: "Yes, there is one thing I will allow you to do for me. You shall teach me that charming ballad you were singing last night; but on this condition, that you tell me where you learned it."

"Was it 'The Man of Ballingry'? No? Or 'Andrew Lambie'? Ah! I know what you mean" (and here I looked upon the ground in my perplexity). "I fear I cannot tell you that. Perhaps it will come to me, but I cannot recall now where I heard it."

"I knew it," she said, indignantly; "I was sure of it. It was very smart of you, but I am not to be taken in by a spy. And now that we understand each other, I shall walk from this part of the garden where we are not seen to that part where we shall be seen, and you may safely go out by the door like a Christian."

"Nay; if I were seen, steps would be taken to prevent my coming here again, and as I purpose to come again, I shall not follow you."

She was now moving away, but she turned, gracefully and coquettishly enough, I will admit, to say:

"Good-bye, Mr. Spy; I should like to see you leap the wall again."

There grew outside the garden wall a beech of gigantic proportions, which had much renown in the district under the name of the Mailer's Tree. This ancient denizen of the Ruthven policies had thrown one of his limbs over the wall and some distance into the garden. Jumping up and seizing the branch at the lowest point which would bear my weight, I drew myself along it hand over hand until I could drop on to the wall; and having made a low obeisance to the lady, who was kind enough to watch the exploit, I dropped into the shrubbery.

Now I conceived not that I had come by the worse in this passage of arms, because it suggested some explanation to me. His Highness was aware of my coming to Scotland, but I could not bring myself to believe that his Chancellor was privy to it. An underhand attempt had been made upon me at Fastcastle, as I believed at the instigation of the Chancellor; but he was a man who did many violent things on suspicion. Yet at first sight it was scarce to be explained why his Highness, who had brought me home, should consign me to the man from whom, above all, he must wish to conceal his purpose.

I knew him, however, to be a very secret and cunning man; and it was possible that, in order to lull the suspicions which his Chancellor seemed to hold about me, he had held back from all communication with me, and had committed me to a castle in Arran's keeping. What if, in appearing to humor the Chancellor, he had sent me to the very place he all along meant to despatch me to? What if the secret lay in this castle? I bit my lips with vexation to think that this was all surmise, and that I had neither information nor instructions.

CHAPTER IV

WELL, I knew that if anybody could tell me what was going on in Ruthven Castle that man lived in Perth, and was the minister of Tibbermure. For the ministry knew not only the scandal of the ale-house and the barber's shop, but a good deal more, and some of the worthy men spent the greater portion of their time in investigating the private misdeeds of their flocks. Never did priest, with the mark of the Beast upon him, ride the people so hard. Master Patrick Murray, though he had no great stomach for this work, knew all that went on in his parish, for there were sundry who would not suffer him to be ignorant.

From him I learned—for I had the means to make him speak — that the Earl of Arran was both hated and feared by the ministry and the people, and that very little was required to make the whole country rise against him. The people hated him for the execution of the Earl of Gowrie, and the Kirk for the persecution it endured at his hands. When the harvest failed, and the infection of Plague grew very sore, men knew that my Lord of Arran was without excuse and past praying for.

As for the young lady kept close at Ruthven, she was the daughter of George Uchiltrie, of Newton, who had been very great with the Regent Morton. Rightly or wrongly, all men believed that the Regent had made great secret hoards of treasure, and that George Uchiltrie knew where they were. So, when the Regent was beheaded, Uchiltrie was booted by the orders of Captain James Stewart, otherwise the Earl of Arran, albeit without any shadow of law. But whether it was that the popular voice was wrong, and the Regent had no secret hoards, George Uchiltrie said never a word. The Raid of Ruthven then put the Earl of Arran from Court for a time, but he came back— and the day arrived when the Laird of Newton simply disappeared from the face of God's earth. He was riding home from the Queensferry when he had word that the passes through the hills were beset for him. He then attempted to cross from Alva to Blackford, a wild road, and rough for horses. As his party skirted the shoulder of Benbuck he found that they were pursued, and, directing them to continue on their way, he turned himself some other gate. From that day

nothing had been heard either of him or his
horse, and most had given him up for dead—indeed, there could be no reasonable doubt that he
was dead.

Thereupon there had been a great rivalry between the Earl of Arran and his brother the
Colonel for the wardship of George Uchiltrie's
daughter. Nobody knew how the matter stood,
although the Earl and Countess had carried the
girl about with them to Edinburgh and Kinneil;
but lately, for what reason was not known, she
had been sent to Ruthven, and in some manner
confined in the castle.

"And now," said the worthy Master Patrick,
"that I have answered your questions, I would
ask a favor of you in return."

"You may take it for granted," I replied;
"what may it be?"

"Well, I would have you attend the sermon
at St. Serf's Chapel, which stands on the other
side of Almond, and tell me what you think
thereof. There came one hither no great time
ago of whom I would have assurance. The
brethren tell me that his ministrations at St.
Serf's smell of grace, but I mistrust me of him."

"What like is he, sir?"

"A fiery-faced, boastful-looking man."

"Calling himself Mr. Peter Wilkie?"

"The very same; but who he may truly be no one here knows."

"Well," said I, "I have seen your man. As I rode through the Hilton of Mailer, on my arrival in these parts from Edinburgh, I noticed a person of ministerial appearance whose face seemed familiar to me. So much was I struck with him that I made inquiry, and was told that he was Mr. Wilkie, of St. Serf's, a very powerful and sanctified 'veshel' when in the pulpit. But though I know not the name of Wilkie, I know the face of that man."

I had looked to be without the presence of Barabbas on this occasion, for the Plague was very sore in Perth, and the people of the neighboring villages were shy of going into the town. But I suppose the Fiend had so inoculated the man with evil that he feared not a hundred plagues, and I had to put up with his company. I brought, of course, both of my own men with me, because the state of the country was such that one with a plack piece in his pocket might not go a mile unaccompanied without danger. We had nearly reached the castle on our return when, from one of those subtle channels of inspiration which the wit of man cannot follow, I became aware that something was amiss.

I was roused from this uneasy feeling by Barabbas, who, pressing past me without ceremony, threw himself from his horse and ran towards the door in the garden wall. This door had been kept carefully closed since I came to the castle, and had the appearance of not having been used for some considerable time before that. It was now open, and marvelling not less than Barabbas at the sight, I also leaped from my horse and ran into the garden. Here was a state of things which puzzled me. On one side Barabbas, having his drawn sword in his hand, was pressing matters with two men, who appeared to be more anxious to drive him off than hurt him. On the other hand were Jean Uchiltrie and her woman, whom a cavalier booted and spurred was addressing in a resolute manner, but with a certain amount of deference. The girl was listening with a contemptuous air, but her woman seemed to be quite unconcerned.

Now I was not going to draw my sword for Barabbas, whose very face I loathed. Nor did I intend to draw readily for the young lady who had a few hours before called me a spy. So, walking towards the latter group near enough to see and hear what was being done, I stood by as one that pauses at a street scene from idle curiosity. Two things, however, I noted carefully—that the sun should be, and the open door of the garden should not be, at my back.

"Madame," the cavalier was saying, "I have treated you with all possible forbearance; but if you will persist in refusing to come, I must summon those who will not be so gentle."

"Summon them," said the girl, with a scornful laugh; "there are also those who will perhaps not treat you as gently as I have."

I know not whether this was intended as an appeal to me, but she looked in my direction, and I returned the look as if I had no understanding of such meaning. Following her eyes, my cavalier turned and saw me.

"Ah!" said he, "madame thinks that this gentleman— May I ask, sir, what you do here?"

"Have you any objection to my being here?" I answered, with indolence, flicking the heads off the gowans with my wand.

"None, so long as you keep your tongue and your hands to yourself."

"Thank you. You will, however, allow me to mind my own business. If not, I may be tempted to inquire into yours."

"Go pack, knave, or I shall take thee by the nose!" he cried, angrily, thinking to bear me down with great words.

"Not so, until I know whether it is this lady's

wish to go with you or not. I had no intention, when I came in, of interfering with what seemed not to concern me. But when an ill-bred cur is not content to worry his bone in peace, but snarls at me, I generally give him something for his compliment."

Again he called upon me to stand from the way, and reaching forth his hand caught the girl by the wrist, in order to drag her towards the gate. He had no sooner done this than I cut him across the ear with the horse-wand which I still carried. Knowing what this meant between men accustomed to carry weapons in their hands, I dropped my wand at once and drew my rapier, making sure at the same time that my dagger was loose. My man was nearly as quick. Coarse wretch that he was, he belonged to a class of men who were ready with their hands and knew no fear. The stroke of the wand had been severe, but well I knew it was the indignity which galled him.

Before one might have counted three, he had dropped the girl's wrist, drawn his sword, and sprung upon me. Like all men whose temper becomes ungovernable, he thought to carry off the matter on the first intention—a thing which does sometimes come about, though not often. Now I had no mind to spare this man; and, moreover, though I have heard men speak of fighting on the defensive, I have never been able to find any system of single combat with deadly weapons which could be so called. But in truth I have known men fight in such a manner that success was impossible. So I stood firmly on my feet, without budging an inch, and, parrying his stroke, nipped him on the forearm before he could recover. I was under this disadvantage, that whereas I wore my corselet, he had on both breastplate and back, and I was forced to play with precision for the vulnerable points.

At an early point in the encounter I noticed— as one will notice trifles at critical moments—a vegetable, such as a leek, which had been dropped on the grass and flattened by somebody's heel. I shifted my ground in order to avoid this hazard of the green; but my adversary in his heat was less cautious, and, after parrying with difficulty a thrust which grazed the outside of his upper arm, he stepped upon the leek, and fell all his length upon his back.

As this was not a combat of honor, but an unwarrantable attack upon myself, I thought at first of putting my foot on his sword; but a deep guffaw from behind telling me that Carryg had come in, it seemed that I needed not to put myself to the trouble. The two fellows who had

beset Barabbas left him when they found that
their master was engaged with me, but the entry
of my men at the same moment had compelled
them to stand by without interference. They
now set him upon his legs, for, having his armor
on, he had got something of a shock by his fall.

"May the devil burst me," he spluttered, "if
I do not have the best blood in your body for
this !"

"Don't be a fool, man," I replied; "I found
you doing something very questionable in this
garden, for I take it you had no authority for
carrying off this lady; and I must tell you now
very plainly that, if you do not clear off at once,
both you and your men shall hang from you
beech-tree within the hour. And an ugly sight
you'll be."

"You have no right to ask for my authority,"
he grumbled; "but," he added, maliciously, "you
may read it for yourself, so long as you show it
not to others." He thereupon handed me a paper, which I proceeded to glance at. It contained authority to Roger Algate to search all
apartments in Ruthven Castle, and, if necessary,
carry away with him such persons as he might
suspect of concealing from him certain jewels
which had been stolen from the royal jewel-chest
in Edinburgh Castle. The paper purported to

be signed by "Arran"; but as it was plainly written in the handwriting of a woman, I laughed softly, and began to fold it up as if to return it.

"Roger, Roger," I said, "I fear you are a very sad and a very bad dog. I wouldn't prevent your having a sweetheart on the other side of the Tweed, but—ah, you rogue!—you shouldn't flourish about your mistress's love-letters as authority for carrying decent women out of their houses. Fie! Roger." And tearing the paper to pieces, I cast the fragments upon the wind, which carried them hither and thither, some over the wall, and some into the trees and bushes.

Thereupon methought Roger would have betaken him again to his sword; but one crying to us from the open gate to "have a bishop in," a little laugh began among our rascals. A number of countrymen coming from the fields, hearing raised voices in the garden and seeing the gate open, had peered in to spy what was going forward. There was not one of those men who had not more or less knowledge of arms, and at sight of them Roger knew that his venture had miscarried, and that if he did not go at once he might not have the chance of going at all.

"For this," he said, with some spite, "you will have to answer to one who will know how to deal with you. If you survive that, you will have to reckon with me."

"Not again with you, Roger," I replied; "next time, if he pleases, another will amuse you, and a pretty mess he will make of you."

Without further words he drew off with his men. Once outside the garden he made for the thicket which grows close by, followed by the country people, who jeered and jested at his expense. He had left two men in the thicket with his horses, but as there were seven horses among five men, it was reasonable to suppose that they came with the fixed intention of carrying off the girl and her woman. Their plan had been good enough. They had been waiting this opportunity for some days in Methven Wood, a natural forest, which was allowed to flourish for the express purpose of harboring broken men, common thieves, and traitors and vagabonds, coming both from the Highlands and Lowlands. On my departure to visit the minister of Tibbermure, by means of a pretended summons from Barabbas they drew off to Forteviot Kirk the three or four men left at Ruthven. Whether by first scaling the wall and removing the bolts, or with the assistance of an accomplice inside, they entered by the garden gate, and, proceeding to the house, searched the whole of Jean Uchiltrie's apartments. But not finding what they wanted, they came to the conclusion that she carried it upon her person.

I had but too much cause to fear that this raid, strange as it might seem, was instigated on the part of the Earl of Arran. The Countess, as everybody knew, had forced the king's jewel-chest; and, when Sir Robert Melvill had the locks altered, she had a new set of keys made for her own use. Whether it was one of the king's jewels or not, it was clear that something of interest was missing, and that Jean Uchiltrie was suspected. For Roger and his men had searched in sober earnest. He could not venture to search the young lady in Ruthven Castle; but there were places near at hand in the High-land glens where that could be done without in-convenience, and without the victim's knowing at whose instance, or even where, it was done. I have little doubt now that such was the inten-tion, and that the unhappy girl had been sent to Ruthven because the place was convenient for executing the scheme. For I afterwards learned that at this time my Lord of Arran went for some days upon a secret journey, and that it was thought—although none knew—that he had gone into the Highlands to buy the interest of some of the chiefs.

In the meantime it occurred to me that, having gained admission to the garden by the door, I was not going to be expelled without knowing the reason. Moreover, friend Roger's authority had given me a clew to Mistress Jean's secret, although she knew not what the paper contained. So, begging a word in private, I prevailed upon her to walk a few paces apart with me. When out of hearing, I faced her, and, looking her gravely in the face, said:

"Where is it?"

"Where is what? What do you mean?"

"It is not necessary to say more—you understand—what your friends, who were here just now, were looking for."

"Looking for? It is true they turned everything upsidedown in the house; but that was but a pretext for carrying off my woman and myself. You know, Captain Eviot, such things are done for less attractive merchandise than I am."

"I am sorry," I said, seriously, "you should take this tone with me. You know as well as I do what Roger Algate came to seek; you know who sent him; you know that, failing to find what he wanted, he was about to carry you off to a place where you yourself might be searched. You were entirely at his mercy but for my inter-

4

ference, and now you deny to me what even the knave himself admitted." I spoke at a venture, but I knew that I was warm.

"Here's a pretty man!" cried she. "Cristine! here, Cristine, is one who swears we carry about with us I know not what, and has a mind to search us himself, as I think."

"I can promise him a good clawing if he begins," said Cristine.

"The man is crazed. I marvel who could have possessed his brain with such maggots."

"Shall I tell you who?" said I; but giving no answer to this, she walked off towards the house. However, when she had reached the flight of steps which led to the first floor, she left Cristine, and, coming quickly back to me, said:

"Who told you this—this nonsense?"

"You might have asked that a little sooner, Mistress Jean. Who told me? Who but Ye Ken Wha?"

"Ye Ken Wha?" she answered, irritably; "oh yes, Ye Ken Wha; but if there be any such person, what did he say?"

"Mistress Jean, as you are pleased to mind your own business, I am moved to mind mine, though this may not be pleasing to the person I have spoken of."

This I said because, although I was what is

called warm, I could not insist further without betraying my ignorance, and finally forfeiting the confidence of this girl.

"Ah," she replied, " I had begun to be sorry for what I said this morning, but now I fear I was right. You seem to think you have obliged me by driving off that wretched man. Who told you that? Was it Ye Ken Wha? How do you know that I prefer to be patronized by you to being carried off by Roger Algate? And, pray, after all is said, what did you do for me? It's easy fighting where your adversary lies down on his back."

"Well, well, the next time I see you in the clutches of Roger I will let you be."

"Nay, Captain Andrew, but you will do exactly as I tell you. Think you I know you not? Why " (and she spoke in a low voice, putting her face close to mine), "you would sooner see the little finger of Jean Uchiltrie than a regiment of other women. But you! What are you to me?" And, snapping her fingers at me with great contempt, she rejoined Cristine and entered the house.

I laughed heartily at this, and said to myself it was not so. And it was not.

CHAPTER V

THE following morning, being the day of the weekly sermon, I betook myself, without much hope of edification, to the chapel in which Mr. Peter Wilkie ministered. For myself, I was of the "Trew Religion," and did not wish to see the order of Bishops revived in Scotland—so far I was sound. My only quarrel with the Bishops was that the Scots neither liked them nor needed them. But the ordering of these matters had fallen into the hands of Mr. Andrew Melvill, who proved to be a "sair sanct" for the Kirk; because with him began the hatred, malice, and uncharitableness which lie between her and the civil power to this day.

Mr. Andrew was a man of great learning and abilities, and very upright in his walk and conversation; but he was a fain and foolish man to lead the Kirk. He taught the ministry that the order of Bishops was not only not meet, but unlawful according to the Scriptures, and damnable; and under his control the Kirk proceeded to claim an interference in civil affairs which no system of government and no race of people could tolerate. It portended a tyranny which would have gone far beyond that of Rome. The King, who was but a boy, though shrewd for his years, saw the encroachments upon the civil power, and retaliated with expedients which endangered the liberties of the Kirk. Much injustice has been done upon this head to my master; for, whatever may be the merits of our troubles now, I do not doubt that he would then have given the Kirk all that it could fairly ask. But the demands made upon him were beyond all reason, and they were put forward by Mr. Andrew and his imitators of inferior mould with such terms of insult and abuse as were not tolerable. Hence he became suspicious; nor do I believe that the Kirk will recover what it has lost through these worthy but unwise men for many years to come.

A sermon from Mr. Andrew Melvill was one thing, the discourse of Mr. Peter Wilkie another. If Mr. Andrew was indiscreet, overbearing, and unfair, his wit and learning were inexhaustible, and he was full of fire. But Mr. Peter? Well, there were but a handful of men, there were no young men, in his congregation; three-fourths of those who attended the sermon were women. Mr. Peter himself, a thick-necked, black-browed man, I had no difficulty in recognizing as having

been in one of our Scots companies at Ghent. I
had also seen him more recently at Edinburgh,
for my host of Robertson's Inns pointed to him,
and told me that some years before he had stood
in the pillory for four hours and was pelted by
the Rascal with rotten fish for saying Mass in the
Kowgate. But then he was no Peter Wilkie.
To what end he supplied this double character I
know not; but that he continued it I do know,
for many years afterwards he was denounced by
proclamation for his abominable atheism in the
same.

In his sermon he first made some bald remarks
upon the text, which were followed by what he
called doctrine. Doctrine it may have been; he
used some very hard words.

But the practical application was the mainstay
of his discourse; and when he arrived at that
there was a shuffling of feet, and the congregation pulled itself together. After some parochial
personalities, we had for grace what in truth I
can only describe as a red-hot picture of hell,
with the King and his Council occupying a
prominent place in the foreground. At times a
few of the women groaned, but the blasphemous
abuse excited no admiration, for, indeed, it had
furnished the greater part of some men's sermons
for two or three years before.

I was presently glad of my knowledge of the man, for by degrees he began to direct his course to me. In the end, pointing with his finger, he cried out at me with great passion:

"Pestiferous traffickers, practeesers, Jesuits, Seminary Priests, and other children of the Antichrist, are creeping into the country, and in this kirk itself sit those who dwell in the portion of Sathan."

As these words drew the eyes of the congregation upon me, I rose at once to my feet and answered him.

"Sir," said I, "you will be good enough to keep your sour tongue off me. I have those to answer for me who know that I am a better servant of the Kirk than you; and for one who has stood in the pillory for saying the filthy and blasphemous Mass in the Kowgate of Edinburgh—"

"Nay, brother," he broke in, sharply, "I did but speak in general terms, and had no thought of touching your particular affairs. I spoke of their famous Archbishop and his minions—the carnal atheists, foul and bloody idolaters, hellish witches, licentious libertines, pernicious flatterers, and such other devilish counsellors—"

"Haud ye there, man," said a hoarse voice near the door, "I canna do wi' mair nor that."

"Peace, mocker; depart, blasphemer, to your
master Sathan. But what can be expected from
such as you, when many of those appointed to
preach the Word of God are found to be festered
and cankered with avarice, lying, deceit, villany,
hand-shaking with bloody murderers, sacrilege,
witchcraft, simony, flattery, apostasy, tricking,
obscenity—"

"God's mercy," whispered a half-witted woman who sat to my left, "I never kenned there
were sa mony deidly sins."

"Wheesht, woman," replied her neighbor, "a'
they sins is amang the Ministers themselves."
The preacher, as if intoxicated by his own powers of abuse—for which he was greatly indebted,
be it confessed, to Mr. Andrew and Mr. James—
went on to touch upon the King, whom he
qualified as a "false, deceitful, greedy smayk,
that smothered and held down the Word of
God."

"Come down!" cried a voice of thunder from
the door of the chapel. "Come down at once,
you white-livered, lying knave." A tall man,
armed with sword and dagger, and a pair of pis-
tolets at his belt, stood between the people and
the light streaming through the doorway.

"I will not come down," bellowed Mr. Peter,
"though all the lions in hell were to roar at me;

and whether you are commissioned hither by God's silly vassal, or the Lady Jezabel, who—"

There was a clanking of steel and a rush, and the tall man, clearing the space between the door and the pulpit, ran up the steps on one side as the pastor fled down the other side and rushed into the vestry.

In a few seconds we were all out in the kirk-yard. The stranger was holding his sword by the scabbard and shaking the hilt of it at Mr. Peter, who stood at a safe distance without the wall. The women made haste to follow him, and minister such consolation as they might. But the men remaining, one of them made so bold as to put his hand upon the stranger's arm.

"And wha may ye be?" said he.

"I," replied the stranger, with a curious smile—"I am Captain James."

Thereupon there was a silence, and in the space of a few seconds Mr. Peter's congregation, male and female, melted away, leaving the intruder and myself alone in the kirk-yard; for the fear of this man's name was as great among the humble as it was among the noble and rich. Assuredly this James Stewart, "callit Earl of Arran," as men say now that he is under the ground, was a man of grand presence. Tall, of great strength, and brought up from his youth to arms, he held

himself above the jests of the insolent or the prov-
ocation of bullies.   His countenance was very
noble; his nose straight and delicate; his hair
inclining to fair with a shade of golden; his
eyes light blue. If a fault could be found with
him, it was in the haughty and imperious expression—which somewhat became him—and the
hardness at the corners of his mouth. But he
had the brave appearance of a man at his prime,
who has been bred both to arms and the manners of the Court. His dress, though rich, was
sober in color, and the dust on his boots and
arms showed that he had but recently come off
the road. Addressing me very gravely and with
much courtesy, he said:

"What think ye, sir, of this?"

"I would, my lord, that I had not come back
to the old country to look upon such scenes."

"Aye, Captain Andrew, it would have been
better for you; you see, although your face and
figure are not known to me, I had no difficulty in finding you. I learned at the castle
that you were here, and as I had that which I
wished to say to you I followed you. But one
moment to close this treason - hole, and as our
roads lie in the same direction I shall be glad of
your company."

He then carefully locked the doors of the

chapel, and, putting the irons in his pocket, came back to me. But as I turned towards the road by which I came, he put forth his hand and stayed me.

"Nay," said he; "let us cross the river higher up. When I am lightly accompanied I return from no place by the road I take in coming. I said, sir, that it might be better for you not to be in Scotland; but that hangs upon what you mean to do. Now I will be frank with you, for you are reputed to be an honest man, as well as a soldier and courtier. You must have seen enough of this country to know that no man is safe in it without taking one part or another."

"I know not that," said I; "I have nothing that men may covet, and I confess the divisions in the State are so strange that I understand them not."

"No; you are scarce so simple as that. It is the Peregrine Ministers and Banished Lords in England against the Earl of Arran; but, by the body of God! I will break them all. Not a Minister or Lord of the whole pack shall cross the Border but his head leaps from his shoulders. All this would have been at an end long ago but for the she-devil who sits and fumes and frets upon the English throne. She has kept these rebels in Newcastle and Berwick, at the King's nose, these twelve months past."

" You have heavy metal against you, my lord. You have put the Kirk against you; and though I am neither for Paul nor Apollos, for Mr. Andrew nor the Bishop, you have been very sore upon the Saints."

"The Saints! the long-faced, canting hypocrites. Why, I undertook to give them every satisfaction. I attended their long, dreary discourses, I listened without murmuring to the abuse they poured upon me from the pulpit, I winked at their treason and blasphemy. I actually did penance in the presence of the King— the stool of repentance, Captain Andrew—I, the first man in the kingdom after his Majesty. And they would none of me. It came to be a question whether Mr. Andrew or I was to go. So I got ready a comfortable chamber in Blackness Castle, with the boots handy, and took care that he had news of what I was doing. As I expected, he found about that time that he had occasion to visit the godly, if there be any, at Oxford and Cambridge."

I knew that this man was playing a desperate game. In every quarter he was making interest to meet the dangers which threatened him. Now it was the French Court, now the Earl of Both-

well and Lord Maxwell, or some of the Highland
chieftains; and again he did his very best to win
the good-will of the Queen of England. Without the last, I well know, his failure was only a
question of time.

"Now, Eviot," he resumed, "what I want at
this moment, and what I cannot find, is an honest man. Believe me, there is not such a man in
Scotland, if it be not the Earl of March, who is a
fool, or Sir James Melvill, who is an obstinate,
officious meddler. I have some men like Adam
Hepburn, Monro, and Colin Ramsay, whom I
knew in the old days in France and the Low
Countries. They will be faithful enough so long
as their hiring lasts, but they would sell me to
the devil for a groat when it ends. His Majesty
has need of men of a different kind. You have
no objection to serve his Majesty?"

"None whatever," said I, well knowing what
he meant; "it was the hope that I might serve
him which brought me home; but I would fain
have speech with his Majesty, and with your
permission I will ride over to Falkland to-
morrow, and petition him for a release from my
ward."

At this the Earl shook his head gravely.

"I should hardly advise that. I will speak to
him myself; and yet—and yet it might be better

so. I need not tell you that he who serves the King serves me."

To this I bowed; but I thought to myself that the King might tell a very different tale if he chose.

So far I had nothing but soft words from the Chancellor. Not a word about the scuffle at Fastcastle, or the tearing up of Roger Algate's warrant, which, I never doubted, was the work of the Countess. But I knew the man's character well by reputation. My life was not worth a minute's purchase if he thought that I balked him in the meanest wish; but he would entertain me with kind words for a space, though he meant the worst. I was keen to be off to Falkland. I would start early the following morning, and—said I to myself—not all the kings in Christendom will send me back to this man.

We parted within the yard of the castle, and I went within to my apartment, wondering whether Mr. Peter Wilkie was an avenging angel or the mean, malignant churl he seemed to me—whether the Earl of Arran really meant me mischief—whether I should ever reach Falkland—and if I did, what the King would say to me—or whether he might not altogether refuse to see me. What was that? Was it not— Yes; somebody was in my chamber. And greatly indeed did I marvel when I saw that two women were busied with my humble possessions. One was on her knees, throwing them out and sifting them ; the other, who carefully handled each article, was a woman of very great presence, a Juno in form and face, though too much inclined to flesh. The lips, however, were full and sensual, and albeit she was handsome, there was an impression in the features of greed and selfishness which women who are greedy and selfish can seldom conceal.

Truly the Ministers were right when they said that Captain James was well mated, for this was the Countess of Arran.

CHAPTER VI

" A BLACK camlet jacket—new; a satin doublet; a riding-coat guarded with velvet. A pretty man indeed! If I could but find some item of Popery in the *pochette* — for I shall find nothing else. Where does the man carry his money? Ah—"

O Monstrous Regiment, is nothing sacred from your claws? Is there no secret into which your eager eyes will not pry?

The woman who took so much freedom with my wardrobe was reputed the most impudent and shameless in Scotland—and that is to say not a little. She disposed of her second and married her third husband under circumstances which were not usual; but she flinched not from them. Nor did she scruple to undergo the penance prescribed by the Kirk, though she gave many grievous words that she, being the daughter of an ancient house, should be moved to humble herself in public. Now she had her revenge upon the Kirk; but if the Earl of Arran ever had hope of success in Scotland, the cruelty, greed, and rapacity of the Countess had surely

quenched it. On all sides she extorted money;
and my poor treasure had not escaped her
clutches but that I carried with me—and that
upon my person—only what I required for immediate use. For a moment she was taken aback,
and lost her speech.

"Madame does me too much honor," said I,
bowing low; "and there is not one of these poor
possessions which will not have a double value
for me, now that they have passed through madame's hands."

"There is more sense in that, sir, than you
think for; for I have washed my hands in the
Hole of Ruthven, the water of which is of virtue
against the Pest. But in truth I am here on
another errand. Having no assurance of you,
Captain Eviot, or your presence here, I took upon
hand to see that you brought with you neither
book, writing, nor monument of Papistry. I
might have directed Rynian, who is a ryper or
licensed searcher, to do this office—which, be you
sure, is not grateful—but having regard for you,
I have undertaken it myself."

"I trust Madame the Countess is satisfied with
what she has seen."

"More or less. Your copy of the Scripture
does not bear as much witness of use as might
be wished; and some part of your wardrobe in-

dicates a sad leaning to the vain show of the world. But be frank with me, Captain Andrew" (here she came close to me, laying her hand upon my arm), "and you will not regret it. What made his Majesty send you here?"

"I only wish I could tell you," said I, throwing my arms abroad.

"Then," replied she, with an incredulous sneer, "you neither know nor guess the reason?"

"I have not the wildest conception of what it all means."

"So be it; but at least you can answer a blunt question—who pays you?"

"Blunt indeed and deficient," said I, with a contemptuous laugh, for I was provoked for the moment, and I felt the blood mount to my throat. I think she saw that she had lost her way.

"Well, who pays for all this?" she retorted, pointing to my scattered wardrobe. "You have two men and three horses here. How is it all done? If you do it on your own means, you may at least say who can answer for it." The fiend had put her finger upon the weakest point of my position. I had a letter of credit to a merchant in Edinburgh from Antwerp; but to name him to this harpy was to lose every groat I had in the world. She sold for hard cash every suit which came before the Council or the Session, and complaints were manufactured by the score in order that the victims of them should buy them off through her. I was in her hands for the moment; but as she did not veil her hostility to me, to make a stand here could not make matters worse.

"Madame will pardon me," said I; "but the name of the person who is answerable for my means is a matter between him and myself."

"Ah! is it so you answer us? We shall see by to-morrow. For the present I will hope that you prove not the busy and dangerous trafficker you are said to be." And so, with a stiff inclination of the head, she descended the turnpike stair, which was indeed the only means of access to my apartment.

What happened thereafter I will set down with some circumstance, because part thereof, and part only, becoming known to sundry in that country, a romance grew upon it which did some injustice to those who deserved it not.

Having given directions for an early start on the following morning, I sat within my chamber searching for light without finding it. It seemed that for some cause the Arrans had taken me in suspicion before I landed in Scotland, and strange it was that, although in their hands, they had allowed me to remain unmolested for some weeks. But now they were to be resolved of me one way or another. I thought, too, of Mr. Peter Wilkie. Were he and the Ministers of his kidney in the right, and was I in the wrong? Were they so good, and the rest of us so vile? Were they, as they were never weary of saying, the "best" people; and was humanity to be swept into Paradise by the terrors of fire and brimstone rather than by the love of God?

Finding to my hand the Book which, the Countess truly said, might have shown more traces of use, I opened it in sundry places, and therein I read not that the Gospel of Christ was preached with blasphemous and scurrilous abuse. But it is written in the Book that the Master, who himself knew what was in man, was sent into the world not to judge, but that the world should be saved. And indeed I could find nothing which recalled to me the bellowings of Mr. Peter and his like.

As I sat so thinking something touched me smartly upon the cheek and fell with a faint sound upon the floor. Marvelling what it might be, I sought for it some time without success; but it was not until I groped on hands and knees that I found it under the bent or white grass with which the floor was strewn. A piece of

paper wrapped round a small pebble, which must
have been thrown through the window — and
thrown from the western wing, for the window
was so far from the ground that one could hardly hope to throw into it from below. The
paper was written upon, and this is what I read
in it:

"At ten hours to-night—on the parapet of the
west wing—you shall have that you seek. Turn
to the left when you cross, and go sunways
round the parapet.   J. U."

The handwriting was unknown to me, but the
initials — could they stand for aught but Jean
Uchiltrie? Then, were they genuine, or did they
conceal a trap? I could not tell that the paper
came from Jean Uchiltrie, for I knew not her
writing; and if it came from her, how knew
I that she would not trick me, and what did
she mean? Again, if it were sent by others
in her name, the intention could scarce be
friendly.

I puzzled my brains over this until I was in
a fever of doubt. First I would go, then wild
horses would not make me go; and in that mind
was I when the hour arrived.

Thus, though still unresolved, I went out upon

the battlements, and greatly marvelled to find, what I had never seen before, a substantial plank thrown across and bridging the space—about ten feet—between the parapets of the two wings. The invitation was plain. Was it given by a friend or an enemy?

It could do no harm to test the bridge, and this I did after a time, finding that it was firm, and that at least there was no intention that I should fall into the abyss between the two wings. From testing the bridge to crossing was but a small step; for though there was a fall of sixty feet below me, I had a good head and a sure foot, and the trick was one I had often practised. A ten-foot plank is soon passed.

Once across I made a mistake. I should have held to the left; but so engrossed was my mind that I followed the parapet to the right. After turning the first angle I crept along by the northern side until I came to some steps, which I descended. I then became aware of a light coming from a door or open window within a few feet of me. I was in doubt whether to go back or stay where I was when I was arrested by my lord's voice.

"What is it, Bess? Why are you at this again?"

"'Tis but M'Kuskan Grossok," replied a voice,

which I recognized, "who is helping me to win some light."

"You will be burned, and the rest of us with you, for the rusty, miskenning scoundrel, if you look not how you go."

"Well, you have allowed our man to go to-morrow, and he will never come back."

"Leave him to me, leave him to me; he will never come back."

"Then leave me to find out what I can in my own way. You will not have justice ministrat upon him, and you will not allow him to be booted, although the boots were brought over for the purpose. I confess that I should be sorry that so proper a man were spoiled by the boots, but you know we are quite at large about him."

"Leave him to me, Bess. He will get more than he thinks for if he does not see reason." It seemed to me, judging from the sound, that on this the speaker left the room.

I listened to this without the slightest scruple. I care not for other folk's talk; but when there are words about booting and ministrating justice upon a gentleman—and that gentleman is one's self—well, let those who prefer to be booted save their ears. But I was minded to do more than listen, for, creeping noiselessly forward, I peered through the window.

What I saw was this: The room was lighted by a rag-wicked candle. In the middle of it was a small table, such as men use for playing cards upon, at which an undersized man, with a face like a ferret, was sitting. There was nothing upon the table, although—for what I could see — some figures or designs may have been traced thereon; but the ferret-faced man was gazing attentively at it. The Countess was standing behind him with her face to the wall.

"Do you see her?" said the lady.

"Yes."

"Where is she?"

"In the kirk-yard of Glendevon."

"What is she doing?"

"She is behind the big gravestone, lying on her face on the grass, watching the great trout that lies in the corner of the black pool."

"What does she say?"

"'Banes to the fire, and soul to hell.'"

"Oh yes; I know that. Anything else?"

"Listen—

"'Leap, little loon, across the moon;
Put out the lamp of Heaven.
For devils lurk behind the kirk,
And villains wait to set the gate
Or he rides in Glendevon.'"

I misliked the mention of Glenderon, for I knew it of old for a place which was greatly affected by those who hold communion with Sathan. For the trout in the black pool—'tis said by some that a trout hath but a life of ten years; but the most aged indwellers in the Glen had knowledge of that trout during all their lives, and I can bear witness after a space of twenty years that it is there still.

"I understand not that," said my lady, "and in any case it is not what I want. Have you the cards?"

The weazened man fetched a small box, from which he took a pack of cards, and, selecting about twenty from the pack, began to deal them. His mistress now stood behind him and looked over his shoulder. He first cut the cards and dealt them into two heaps—two cards each time to the left heap and one to the right. He then took them up and dealt them again, reversing the proportion. Finally he dealt every third card into a small heap, and, taking the third card from the top of the heap, turned it over on its face.

"It's Craft," said the Countess, after looking carefully at the card. "James is right, and yet the design is very like the other."

I could see the card from where I crouched,

for the light fell upon it. It bore a design on which were two castles standing together, and the moon was shining upon them. A road leading from the castles and disappearing on the horizon was stained with drops of blood. It was the card known as *La Lune* in the Tarot. As I craned my neck forward to see this precious sight I felt a soft touch on my arm which made my flesh creep. I fairly shivered from head to foot. I dared not turn quickly round, lest I should draw the attention of the persons in the room; if I did not turn, my enemy might strike from behind. I took my chance of the latter risk, and, drawing myself slowly back, turned round to find myself face to face with—Jean Uchiltrie; and for the first time it flashed across my mind that after crossing the plank I should have held to the left.

Without giving time for speech she turned, and, signing to me to follow, remounted the steps with extreme caution. When we were safely on the other side of the building she stopped, and, putting her face very close to mine, in a manner by no means displeasing, said, in a whisper:

"Are you a fool or only a bold man? You never were in greater danger in your life than you have been within the last few minutes. Put

your head down—low—lower." She put her
arms round my neck. I was in a maze of astonishment; I thought she was going to kiss
me. The imperious beauty was going to kiss the
flouted soldier of fortune. But she was not—of
course not; and I was glad and I was sorry
when I found that instead of embracing me she
was simply putting a necklace or a chain round
my neck.

"Now you have it," she said. "Wear it inside
your doublet."

"I will," I murmured; "but what is it?"

"It is the X, of course."

"The X?" I said. "What on earth is that?"

"Are you frenzied, man? Did you not write
yourself and ask me for it?"

"That I can safely say I never did."

"What! you didn't? Then, sir, you will be
good enough to give it back to me."

"Nay," said I; "I shall keep the chain now
that I have it, for I would teach you that I am
worthy of more trust than you have hitherto
given me. But go at once; for, look you, if you
received a missive which purported to come from
me, it is like that a trap has been laid for us.
Ere it be too late I will bid you not good-bye,
but *au revoir.*"

I could not see, and I did not stop to see, the

effect of these words, but hastened back to the plank. I again took the precaution of testing it, and it was well I did so, for no sooner did I put my foot upon it than it slipped from under me and disappeared over the parapet.

CHAPTER VII

THE loss of the plank was a serious matter for me—and others. I had been in haste to return to my own part of the castle, because it was clear that somebody had laid a trap for me or Mistress Jean, or both of us. And now I could not go back at all. The person who had forged the letter in my name had succeeded in part of his object: Jean Uchiltrie had passed the X into my keeping. But he had possibly not thought of the plank bridge, and as yet did not know what had happened. And yet he might be waiting to catch me in an equivocal position; if so, it seemed that he had succeeded, and I was caught like a rat in a trap.

I crept back to the bartizan, where the girl was still watching me.

"Tell me," said I—"this is no time for words, but tell me—what chance is there that I may pass through the house unseen?"

"Absolutely none. You must pass through the rooms on the first floor, where are my Lord of Arran's men. If you took them by surprise you might make a push for it; that is your best, your only, course. You don't know those people as I do or you would know that. If you are found here you will be pitched over the battlement without more ado, and no questions asked. Draw your sword, sir, I say, and commit you to God."

"No, no, Mistress Jean; that would be but a forlorn - hope at the best, and I must think of others. I must not be seen here, and there is but one way for that. See, it is but ten feet from here to the keep."

"For the love of God think not of that; it is certain death."

I thought differently. A ten-foot jump is no great matter, even without a run, but there were circumstances which made this leap more perilous than even Jean Uchiltrie thought. The parapet upon which we stood was two or three feet lower than the parapet of the keep, so that when the plank was thrown across one end of it rested upon the parapet of the keep and the other end upon the roof of the western wing, at a point some feet above the parapet. How this end of the plank had become dislodged from its position on the roof I could not tell. But it was clear enough that, if I attempted to leap, I should have to jump upward, and that, as the parapet of the keep was higher by three feet, I could not make a clean jump of it. My only hope was that I might land so as to grip the top of the parapet with my arms.

I examined the place with great care, and finding that the two buildings were not exactly parallel, but that they diverged towards the north, and approached each other at their southern ends, I chose a spot at the narrowest point. Mounting here, with my left foot upon the top of the parapet and my right upon the roof, I measured the distance and elevation with my eye, and made my spring.

I landed well and according to my calculation, but just before my arms gripped the parapet my foot struck against something—I missed my hold and fell. As I fell I caught—as a drowning man catches—at the parapet, and my hand grasped one of the gutters which protruded just above the corbels. It was doubtless against this object that my foot had struck ; and, as it had destroyed me a second before, so now it gave me life—for a few moments. It was but a slender thing to bear my weight, and I knew I could not cling long to it. I tried to raise myself and reach the top of the parapet with my hand, but I failed. I tried again, and failed. Then I knew I was done, and my weight upon the gutter seemed to double. It was but a few seconds to wait, and I should be falling down — down. I thought of the girl, who, I knew, was watching me but ten feet away, and who, in her anxiety not to unnerve me, had not uttered a sound.

I was beginning to grow dazed when I heard a small, soft voice behind me — it seemed to speak in my ear:

" Turn your face to the left."

Up to that point I had hung with my face towards the south. I now turned mechanically to the north, and saw the lost plank hanging by a rope within eighteen inches of me. I remember noticing, when I first saw it, that a rope with a noose was attached to my end of it. Without any conscious purpose I had passed the noose over a projection of the battlement, and the result was that, when the farther end of the plank slipped off the roof of the west wing, the plank itself was suspended by the rope from the parapet of the keep.

I was now very much exhausted, but I was able to shift my hands to the rope, and could coil my legs round the plank, and that done I was a new man. I was soon out of danger, with the loss of a few inches of skin from my knuckles; but, indeed, at the moment I would readily have given the knuckles themselves of both my hands in return for my life.

I leaned against the doorway in the roof incapable of speech, and the girl still stood watching me from the other side of the chasm. Quickly gathering for what she waited, I drew up the plank, and poised it again upon the opposite roof, whence she bore it away to its own place.

All this passed quickly ; but my absence from the keep even for a quarter of an hour might have drawn some attention to what was happening. I found no, sign of this in my own room ; but it was well I had not lingered, for I had no sooner washed the blood from my hands and bound them up than I had a visit from no less a person than my Lord himself. If this man knew or had any suspicion of my adventure, he had a rare command of himself. He brought with him a letter for the King, which he begged me to carry with me to Falkland in the morning, inasmuch as he could not attend the Court for a day or two to come.

When he was gone I looked first at the letter, but the exterior bore nothing but these words : "To the King, his most Sacred Majestie." I was grateful for this errand, because it would insure me audience of his Majesty, and I placed the letter carefully within my doublet.

6

But I was eager, above all, to see what manner of necklace Jean Uchiltrie had cast about my neck. I found it to be a chain of massive gold links, an ornament which must have cost a great sum of money. The chain, however, was but a worthless toy compared with the jewel it carried. This jewel was in the shape of an X, or, rather, St. Andrew's Cross. It consisted of nine diamonds or white sapphires of great size and beauty set in gold, with roses of gold between the stones. On the back were the letters $_{SPA}^{SFE}$, but I did not at that time guess what they might signify. I gazed upon it with delight, and, as I was to make an early start in the morning, replaced it within my doublet, where, at all events, it was as safe as my own life. I threw myself upon my pallet; but, being disturbed in my mind by the occurrences of the day, I did not extinguish my candle.

What made the Countess raise the arras in the corner of the room by the turnpike stair? Was she not well called the Lady Jezabel? I liked not this coming to my room by night. I could not suffer that. And she smiled with a kindness which was not familiar to her features. Methought her smile was almost what I pictured to be an angel's. What had wrought this change in the woman? And why should she put her hands upon my neck? Ah! the chain; no, it was not that, for she knew not that I had it: but it was to strangle me, and her hands were strong.

I tried to rise, but I could not move a joint of my body, far less struggle — and I was being killed. After what seemed a long time I awoke: it was a dream, but even so it was some minutes before I could move. The candle had burned out, and the chill morning air came through the window. It was a dream, thank God, and I slept again.

About six hours of the morning I was roused by Carryg, and quickly descended to the castle-yard, simply satisfying myself that the letter and jewel were safe within my doublet. We were a party of four, for Barabbas, according to custom, was one of us. I wore my steel-bonnet and armor, and the other three had lance-staves and plate-sleeves, for I knew now that the strong hand was the law of Scotland, and I did not intend to be cut off—if cut off I must be—without a struggle.

Going easily, for part of the road was very steep, we reached Falkland before noon with but one incident to break the quiet of the ride. After crossing the Earn the road rises gently for a few miles, but the ascent into the Pass of Dron de-

layed us somewhat. As we were coming into
Glenfarg, below the Clochrigstane, we heard far
ahead of us the sound of a horse coming towards
us at a great speed. Presently a cry from the
far side of the valley and above us drew our attention to a rider whom I recognized as one of
my Lord of Arran's men. He pointed as he rode
to the stream where the ford lay between us, and
shouted loudly. Although we saw not the ford
for the trees, I gathered that he was in pursuit
of somebody who was crossing the river. It was
as I thought, for we soon espied a horseman
coming down the hill at full speed.

Not being minded to dip in quarrels which
were none of mine, I drew my horse to one side ;
and, the others following my example, it seemed
that there would be no interference from my
party. But just as the man passed Barabbas
touched his mare with the spur and picked his
man out of the saddle with his lance. Whether
by the fall or the point of the lance the fellow
was, I believe, quite dead ; anyway, he moved
not, but lay as he fell, with the face downward.
He was scarce there before Barabbas dismounted, and, bending over him—though without in
any way moving the body—possessed himself of
everything he had about him—that is to say, of
a whinger, a knife, some string, a coral necklace,

an old horse-comb, a Portugal ducat, two Rose
Nobles, and two pounds of white silver.

"That's bonnily done," said Carryg, who was
much moved by the smartness of the whole trans-
action. "Eh, man, ye will be a ryper."

"Aye," replied Barabbas, "I will be something
of that kind." And with some ostentation he
proceeded to lay out the spoils upon the grass, as
one who would say : "See, I am an honest man ;
I have kept back nothing."

But Barabbas did keep back something which,
in spite of the nimbleness of his hands, I saw
him take from the dead man's doublet. I had
been watching for a hold upon this man, and
now it seemed to me that by-and-by there would
be some conversation between Barabbas and me
about that something—which was nothing more
nor less than a letter. But at this moment his
fellow, who was named Joshua Henderson, coming up, inquired at once whether he had searched
the body.

"For," said he, "it had been an ill day for me
if he had gotten off with his pouch full. What,
man Rynian," he added, as he glanced over the
spoil, "is this a' ye took fra off him ?"

"Aye, is it ; and ye are welcome to your ain
from it, and half of the rest, though it is the spoil
of my spear. Na, na ; ye needna trouble to rype

the poor body again. It's an empty hand that comes after Rusty Rynian's."

"And that's true," said the fellow, with a rueful face; "but had he not my lord's letter that he stole fra me? It was for the Laird of Kilsyth."

"A letter?" replied Barabbas, opening his eyes very wide and whistling; "that's bad. Look ye here, laddie—dinna ye gang back to Captain James wi' yon tale. Ye had best take your foot in your hand, and be off to the Border, where they're aye wanting lang-luggit lads. And I'll make ye a present of the haill of the loon's gear, for ye'll maybe be a day or two on the road. But who was by when he grippit the letter?"

"Nane but he and I and the horses. And whose man he was I canna say, for he carried no mark."

Hereupon I bade the rogues hold their peace and lift the body; so they carried it a few paces from the road, where doubtless it lay unburied for a month.

And so thereafter we came to Falkland, but only to find that the King had unexpectedly ridden to St. Andrews. We had no choice but to follow him, and that we did after resting our horses for a couple of hours.

Now while we waited, the heat of the sun being very great, I put off my back and breast-plate and my gauntlets, and was minded to have spoken with Barabbas but that I could not find him. On putting on my armor again, before remounting, I found an obstruction in my right-hand gauntlet, by reason of which it was not possible to insert my hand. Supposing that this might be something secret, placed there—who knew?—by the King's direction, I made an ex-cuse for re-entering the ale-house, and, passing into the garden behind it, where I was not ob-served, I drew from the gauntlet a ball of crum-pled paper. It consisted of two papers, or, rath-er, letters; the cover which held them was gone, but their contents were to be but too easily un-derstood.

The shorter of the two letters ran thus:

"Maist Wise and Gracious,—I have de-spached unto you the pretty man whom your Hienes consigned to my cair in this Castell. I have fund no use for him heir, but to make him the bearer to your Matie of his own letter which was taken from his messenger twa dayes ago: That so he may be dealt with as seem best to your Maties maist wise and princelie jugement. Hartlie kissing your Mat^{les} hand, and praying the Eternell to grant your Hienes lang lyfe, I rest your maist humble and obedient Servitour.

"JAMES, ERLE OF ARRAN.

"*From the* CASTELL OF RUTHVEN."

If I liked not the look of this, I was somewhat more deeply moved by the following:

"RIGHT TRAIST FRIEND, — I greet you weill. You will receave my news in this letter by a sure hand, and doubtless ere that you will havo receaved by a hand still mair sure that of which you have knawledge; but that you may not doubt my meaning, I will plainly say that I mean the jewell callit the X. I was sent hither to ward by ——, who spoke with me at Holyroodhous, saying much at large as one who had a great conceat of himself. Yet being Davy's son he is but a carle, and his learning some rotten ends of the Law and the Prophets, learnit backwards. But, if I mistake not, what I have sent you will, before many days be out, teach him to think mair cheaply of himselff. From the Castell of Ruthven. Your assured good friend,   ANDREW EVIOT.

" *This* 15 *of June* 1585."

CHAPTER VIII

THESE letters so alarmed me that I was resolute not to go forward until I had pondered
thereupon. The idea occurred to me that they
had been placed in my gauntlet by some mis-
chievous person who desired to put me off my
visit to the King. But I rejected it at once, for
no man would employ so clumsy a means to so
simple an end. I did not doubt that the shorter
note was in my Lord of Arran's hand, and
that he had forged the other in my name, hoping to disgrace me with the King. The contemptuous references to my master's learning,
of which he was justly proud, and to Davy as his
supposed father, were enough to insure me immediate imprisonment and probable execution.
If there was one thing the King could not tolerate it was any reference to the extravagances
of his mother.

I had otherwise good reasons for suspecting
my Lord's intentions. My presence at Ruthven
had apparently annoyed him from the first, although he had been suave and polite in his per-

sonal relations with me. On his own admission,
I had escaped the boots only because he had a
better way of dealing with me. There had also
been an attempt, by means of a forged message,
to bring on a communication between his ward
and myself. In this he had probably acted upon
a mere suspicion that the X was in her hands;
and he had failed in his object only because it
never occurred to him that she would commu-
nicate with me by way of the roof. Forgery
was a weapon often used by this man and by
others; and a very formidable weapon it was
when the roads were dangerous and the wings
of truth slow. These letters were part of his
work, and no doubt he was thinking of them
when he said "leave him to me."

But there was one thing which puzzled me—
who put these letters in my gauntlet? If I were
right he must be a friend—but who was he?
If one of my company did it, that one must be
Barabbas, or Arran's post, who had returned
with us from Glenfarg, for I knew that neither
of my men would do it. If Barabbas—that led
me into a curious puzzle. I had seen Barabbas
take a letter from the dead man's doublet, which
he kept for his own private purpose. Was I to
think that he had opened the packet, and, after
reading the contents, passed them over to me?

That was to suppose some very improbable things, as that he had betrayed his master, and was risking his own neck to oblige me. Besides, there was the word of the post himself that the packet was for the Laird of Kilsyth, while these letters were indubitably for the King's eye.

The solution of this puzzle seemed to come from the letters in my hand. According to Arran, I was to be "the bearer of my own letter, which was taken from my messenger twa days ago;" and, as I was not the bearer of it, the inference seemed irresistible that these letters had been tampered with, or that they had been misdirected by accident. By some mischance the post had been carrying the letter meant for the King to the Laird of Kilsyth—but what was the letter which I carried in my doublet? Was it for the Laird of Kilsyth, and could I safely deliver it to the King?

On the whole, I thought that this letter was more likely to do me good than harm. The other letters had miscarried; and, although I knew my Lord of Arran would begin again, I could take care that that trick was not played upon me a second time. I thought I was safe enough for a day or two, and I was resolved that, unless I found some satisfaction at St. Andrews, I should not again put myself inside the jaws of the lion. These reflections somewhat reassured me; but they delayed me some little time at Falkland, and the afternoon was far advanced when we rode into St. Andrews, and some time was lost in securing a lodging for the night. The King, we found, was in the Auld Inns, which men once called the Prior's House. It stood at no great distance from the tennis-court and the ruins of that great structure which Mr. Knox caused the Rascal to destroy.

It was late in the day to seek admission to the King's presence; but the letter I carried for him gave me an excuse, and some commotion beginning about his lodging at the moment of my arrival helped to procure my admission within the wall surrounding it. A loud calling and shouting arose in the court-yard of the Inns, and thither ran everybody within the enclosure. Drawing near with the rest, I found that the outcry came from a room on the first floor, the window of which was open, the night being very warm. Below this window was a small crowd of about thirty persons—grooms, lackeys, and jackmen—who listened with that face of amused interest which men assume when they stand by and watch the follies of their betters.

There were two voices, both of great power. One deep in tone, with a measured utterance;

the other loud and rapid of speech—the voices
of men bellowing with rage, and striving to
roar each other down. From some of the
words which came out upon the night air I
gathered that both were as powerful in their
language as their lungs. But the strange thing
—the thing which brought the smile to the faces
of the little knot of listeners—was that the subject of dispute was—the Kirk.

"Be moderate, Mr. Andrew," said the deep
voice, "and have some regard to our presence.
If noise would serve, ye'd bear the bell away.
Ye've been gaping for full half an hour, like the
President of a Craws' Court, and making no bet-
ter sound or sense for a' that I can hear."

"I had need to speak loud to ears that hear
not, and hearing do not understand. I speak
boldly in your presence, because I am the mean
messenger of one who is a Prince above you;
and I tell you, sir, that it will pass your power,
or that of any that come after you, to take from
God's Kirk the power of binding and lousing."

"That's aye your sang. Ye can bind or louse
a' the devils in hell if it please ye—the mair the
merrier. But ye would be omnipotent in this
State, and when ye are asked for reason ye say
ye are the messenger of God and not to be ques-
tioned. Why, deil take ye, man, if the Lord has

to answer for a' that ye say and do, He'll be sair
put to it. Your syllogism runs in this wise:
Mr. Andrew is the messenger of God; the authority of God is infallible; therefore the authority of Mr. Andrew is infallible. That's exactly what that auld sneaking sinner the Pope
says of himself, and with mair color of reason;
but whereas he is content to sit upon the Seven
Hills at a convenient distance, ye must needs
clap your hinder parts about the thrapple of
your anointed Prince."

"I would, sir, ye were as free from suspicion
of Papistry as I am. There are strange tales
abroad, and but for them ye had not seen me
here this night. I have your Majesty's safe-conduct; but even with that I would not have faced
the perils of the sea and the malice of your Majesty's familiar friends to come hither but that
I had a testimony to uplift—"

"It's marvellous strange, Mr. Andrew, that ye
are aye troubled wi' a testimony when ye visit
us. I sorely fear it is a Papish testimony, for
ye will have me not above but under ye. *Im-
perator bonus intra, non supra, ecclesiam est*,
saith Ambrose; but ye would read it *infra ecclesiam*. There is not one of the points ye are
sa thrawin about for which ye will not find warrant in the Papist writers. Why, man, Father

Ogilvy, the Seminary Priest, and the whole crew of *boni operarii*, sing the same sang as yourself, note by note."

"And what if they do claim for their filthy religion some rights which are due to the Kirk of God? Does that make it wrang for the Kirk to claim its due? It pities me, sir, that a Prince of your Majesty's learning should be sa stangit with the poison of the Dragon as to use such arguments, which are indeed more fit for bairns."

"And sa indeed thought I when ye quoted a' the Bishop's points out of the Papists. But it seems that we may not grease our mouths in private with the butter that the Principal of the New College slabbers in public. Ye will say, na doubt, that ye are the messenger of God, and not to be judgit by the same measure as the Bishop. But how is it, man, that ye are bauld to excommunicate my Bishop, and have na the sponke to excommunicate me who made him Bishop?"

"We dare do that, too, sir; and I am here to tell ye that we will do it if ye do not repent and put from ye that godless Papist and bloody Haman, callit the Earl of Arran, and his filthy and adulterous spouse, meet match for the devil himself."

"Wheesht, man, wheesht. I promised ye

should be free to come hither and see me in quiet manner, and also to return; but ye ken that in Scotland even the air has lugs of its ain, and I canna answer for ye if such words come to bloody Haman's ears."

"I care not to whose ears they come; for know I not, James Stewart, that you have been trafficking with the Antichrist, and that you carry in your bosom the mark and order of the Beast, which he hath given you to be a sign that you are his?"

"Ye are in the wrang, Mr. Andrew, and presume ower far upon our patience. We have no mark of the Beast upon us. Doubtless ye refer to yon idle bruit about the Jewel callit the X. Weel, we have no such jewel or emblem of Popery about us; by the wounds! man, if such thing exists, we ken not in what part of God's earth it lies. And this we say *in verbo Principis*. So, as it is time ye were aboard, and I fear ye have mair learning than sense, we will adjourn these matters until—"

"Until a mair convenient season. Say it, sir, for I perceive your meaning but over plainly."

"Nay, until God purge ye of impertinent pride. The man is distracted of his senses."

This discussion was listened to, for the most

part, in silence; but there was some tittering, and now and again a tall, dark man, who seemed to be greatly gratified, burst into broad laughter. The disputants, however, if they heard him, were too much occupied with each other to notice his presence.

So the X Jewel was, according to Mr. Andrew Melvill, a Popish emblem—a pretty piece of baggage to carry inside one's doublet. I would fain have had speech with Mr. Andrew, for the man was a great scholar and a good servant of his Master; and I had a testimony to lift up to him on my own account, which, however, would have moved him not a jot. But my business pressed, and it seemed that he would return into England by ship; for his visit was private, and unknown even to his own people in St. Andrews.

Now it is possible that I might not have seen his Majesty that night but for an unforeseen occurrence. Being unable to come at the Colonel Stewart, and my name not being known to those on attendance on the King, I was not able to penetrate beyond a certain hall, which, the space being limited, was used by the gentlemen of the Chamber. Here some efforts were made to induce me to part with the Earl of Arran's letter, but that I positively denied to do. Presently

7

the tall man who had laughed so heartily at the
King's wit came and began to eye me with that
nameless insolence which cannot be described.
In strutting up and down the room he contrived,
whether by accident or of purpose, to rasp the
point of his sword against me; but going closer
by me than he had meant, he received such a
push as sent him with his hands spread out
against the wall.

Hereupon arose some tumult with loud speaking, at which a door leading to the King's
apartments opened, and a marvellously elegant
young gentleman, whose face was unknown to
me, came out.

"What's this?" said he. "Gautric, you ought
to know that his Majesty will not suffer these
disturbances near him. Who is this gentleman?"
and he looked earnestly at me, as if he knew me
not.

"Sir," said I, in reply, "I am Captain Eviot,
and I am here to place in the King's hands a letter from the Earl of Arran; but this gentleman
has borne himself with such insolence towards
me that I turned his face to the wall."

Upon that he repeated the name "Eviot"
twice, as if he were striving to recollect it.
Then having gone again into the King's chamber, he returned in a few moments, and brought

me into the King's presence, where I delivered my letter and was permitted to kiss the King's hand.

His Highness, apparelled in a night-gown of tawny velvet embroidered with gold, was seated on an arm-chair, while one of his gentlemen was engaged in pulling off his boots. But no sooner had he opened the letter than he appeared to be greatly surprised, and glanced at me with a blank, puzzled look. I confess I had reason to be uneasy, but I tried to look as unconscious as possible.

"God's soul and body! man," burst out the King, "what manner of prank is this ye have played on us? See, read your letter to us, if ye can."

I took the letter in my hand, and was astounded to see that the page was blank.

"I knew naught, sir," said I, "of my Lord of Arran's purpose; but, if it please your Majesty, the letter may be written in white ink, and if so the heat of the candle will suffice to show the writing."

"Weel, *fiat experimentum;* but haste ye, Captain Andrew, for our throat is dry with bellowing at yon bull of Bashan."

I drew the paper near to the candle, under the rays of which the writing gradually became distinct, and I was able to read aloud to the King the following letter:

"RIGHT TRAIST FRIEND,— I greet you weill. Having your welfare at heart, I have thought it meet to acquaint you with that which may concern you and all those who ride by the King's stirrup. It is known to some here that there is a practice against the lives and liberty of the King and his Chancellor. The ship is at the Wemyss which shall carry his Highness into England; and the purpose is to seize his person some ten days hence within the Park of Falkland. The Chancellor has had George Drummond of Blair in the boots for this enterprise, and will show the same courtesy to one Eviot, warded these many weeks in Ruthven Castle, who—if all tales be true—could show the whole *pot aux roses*. The King is suspected of some hollow dealing in sending this knaive to an open castle. But he careth not for anything save for dogges and deir. At the Court men cannot close their eyes to sleep, or open their mouths to eat, for continual hunting; and it is weill seen that for a pair of good deir-dogges the Prince would give a score of his Ministers, and throw the Bishop into the bargain.—Yours in the auld manner,

"THOMAS MILLER.

"*This 15 of June 1585.*"

"What deil's gett is yon?" cried the King. "But his last word is no so much amiss, for I ken many an honest hound that is worthy of mair commendation than Craig, or Mr. David Black, and all his sort. Dogs and deer! dogs and deer! Deil stick him!—but think ye, Patrick, that the loon would ken anything about such matters?"

The Master of Gray, the elegant young man who had been pulling off his master's boots and replacing them with pantaffles furnished with thick soles, looked carefully at the letter, and said, quietly:

"I think, sir, it is a jest, though I understand it not. The letter is for the Laird of Kilsyth, but the cover is directed to your Majesty, and the writing is the writing of my Lord of Arran."

"It is even so; awa' wi' it for an unseasoned jest. But we would ask this braw messenger if he hath any knowledge of Beza. Have you read the *Confessio*, man, or the *Tractationes Theologicæ?* Is it so? Then, as the night is warm, we will go below to the garden and speak with you thereon."

So we went down by some stone steps into the garden, which was surrounded by a low wall, and his Highness carried me with him to the centre of the grass, where he seated himself upon a stone bench.

CHAPTER IX

"AND do ye ken, man, Andrew, your errand in this country?"

"Indeed I do not, sir."

"But ye will have some guess of it?"

"Well, sir, I think it hath somewhat to do with one of the Crown-jewels called the X, which has been stolen out of the jewel-chest in the Castle of Edinburgh; but I know not the truth of the matter."

"And no sa bad a guess, for though it be not exact to the mark, I marvel that ye came sa near. I'm thinking the Colonel was not far wrang. It happened to us some time syne to say in hearing of sundry of our Council that we kenned not an honest man in our kingdom of Scotland who was not a fool; and the loons, scarce knowing upon which leg to dance, held their peace. But the Colonel, though he made no claim for himself, rounded in my ear that he kenned ane. 'Is that so?' said I, for I thought that he had some turn to serve in saying it. 'Aye,' answered he, 'nane other than Captain Andrew Eviot, now in the service of the States.' Now the Colonel is but a simple body, and he will do by accident what none of the others would do willingly—whiles he speaks the truth. Sa, though we told him that his honest man was removit to a marvellous distance from our Court, we took heed of what he said, for we have sair need of some honesty about us."

"It was the hope of serving your Majesty that brought me to Scotland."

"I ken that, sir. When ye were brought to me in our Palace of Holyrood I made ye no sign. But I knew ye to be a stanch man, for ye said never a word, nor so much as showed a change of countenance, though you got but uncivil entertainment."

"It was evil likely enough then, and I am no nearer to understanding it now."

"Bide a minute, Captain Andrew, and hear what I have to tell ye. Some time syne a certain chain with a jewel attached came into our keeping and possession, as it were by way of pledge. Though *post 5 et* 100 *proavos invicti manemus*, we are strangely pressed at times for money, and have not the revenues to maintain waged men of war as becometh a Prince. It chanced that our cousin of Spain was in the mind to thrust 20,000 red-hot Papist soldiers into this our realm ; and we were constrained to certain temporary shifts to preserve our independence. So, partly of good-nature, partly to serve some necessity of the moment, we took upon us the pledge of the Jewel callit the X, which was unhonestly subtracted from our cabinet at Holyroodhouse, and is now at large."

"And what like is this jewel, sir ?" said I, being careful not to touch on the flaw in the King's excuse for himself.

"It is a jewel of white sapphires and gold roses ; but it is not, as ye suppose, a Crown-jewel, nor was it ever in the jewel-chest in Edinburgh Castle. Ye would ken it best by the letters $^{SPE}_{SPA}$, which are graven on the back. And it is in these letters that the trouble lies, for little did I knaw, when I took the gear in pledge, that it was a rank monument of Papistry. Ye may judge for yourself what dangers to our service may ensue, not only in Scotland, but with our cousin the Queen of England, if we get not this pledge back into our hands. Already that auld blethering worry-cow, Mr. Andrew Melvill, has smelled out something of this, and if he once had the truth of it I should scarce have a day's rest until the daft body was hangit. Now, sir, I sent ye to Ruthven Castle because I knew ye were safer there than anywhere else in Scotland, and ye were near those who might show ye something of this matter. For to be round, I fear that the jewel hath been taken by the Lady of our Chancellor, who is a thought ower nimble with her fingers when they get among other folks' gear."

"And do I understand, sir," said I, feeling somewhat mortified, "that the recovery of this jewel is all the service you require of me?" So vexed indeed was I that I was minded not to give him the jewel, though it hung at that moment round my neck.

"Is that all, say ye?" cried he, growing warm with choler; "what mair would ye have? Will anything please ye? Here is a matter of State which affects the stability of our Crown, and upon which many great enterprises hang; for, if James Stewart turn Papist, what then, man? We are trusting you with our mind upon this subject; and, though other folk may suspect, you alone have the knowledge of it. Then say ye, Is that all?"

"Surely, sir, this is a service that many here would have done better than I who am a stranger to your Court."

"Ye are in the wrang there. Of all these brave gentlemen ye see about us there is none who—but for fear or interest—would not sell us like a bullock to the highest bidder. And if I had required this service of one of them, he would have had large offers of siller from the Queen of England, or the Duc de Guise, or the Bishop of Ross, or our cousin of Spain—for a' these bodies are as busy as bugs with our maist private matters. The young gentleman yonder, who is pleased to mind our writings for us—he gives copies of everything to Wotton, the English Ambassador; our very cook is not safe from them. But we are weel content that it should be so; for so they think that they have knawledge of all our secret dealings, while we have the assurance that they knaw na mair than we choose. For, man, the King is the only person in Scotland whose secrets are known to nobody. And therefore we are concerned to hear how ye came at sa much knawledge as ye have."

To this long address I replied that I was sorry that the service demanded of me was so simple, but that I could do no less than render it at once. So, bending forward, I caught the chain with both my hands and drew it forth over my head.

Great God! what was this?

Though not conscious of such things at the time, I can see now the sparkle of pleasure in the young King's eye when he understood my gesture. I can see the looks of disappointment, doubt, and suspicion which succeeded; and I can hear his loud laughter, which brought me to the knowledge that I must present a strange spectacle with my open mouth and staring eyes. The X Jewel was gone, and in my hand lay a chain of calcedonies.

From the day my mother brought me into this world of sin and sorrow I can remember no moment of like humiliation and dismay. The earth, had she been kind, would have gaped for me, but she did not.

After a space, when I had caught my breath again, I said :

" Think you, sir, that the devil hath power to do the like of this ?"

" I thought not," replied the King, " that God's Ape would have uttered himself so bauldly within the precincts of our Court. That he hath done such things, himself in the form of a goat-buck, or by other spirits in the likeness of a little beast or fowl, is ower weel kenned to be gainsaid. But I must know something of your story, or I can rightly resolve your question."

So I told him my story from the beginning, and he listened with attention, as well he might, for it concerned him as much as myself. When he interrupted me from time to time his comment was of rare shrewdness for one of his years.

The account of M'Kuskan Grossok and the witch of Glendevon greatly excited him.

"Glendevon, say ye? Saul of God! I like not that. It is an evil place, for all it looks sa bonny in broad daylight, and smiles over the stream as though it feared it not. But by night it is the haunt of rank hell-dogs, and Sathan himself hath ofttimes preached his damnable stuff from the very pulpit which is filled by the minister of God. We had a mind to adventure ourselves in it, to wrestle with him and drive him forth, but the pestilent crew of Puritans would have cried out that we had dealt with the Evil One, sa that for the time the place is sair ridden by witches. I ken not what concern this chiel — Grossok ca' ye him? — hath in the place; but women are aye ready to deal with witches for every little trifling turn they have ado with."

When I came to the dream or vision which troubled me the last night I was at Ruthven Castle he said that doubtless I had been ridden by the Mare or Incubus, and that my senses were dimmed by "a thick fleume."

"And yet, man," he added, after appearing to consider my figure for some seconds, "it fears me that ye had mair commerce with the Lady Potiphar than the Lady Jezabel. Have ye told me all, or are ye keeping back ony part of the tale, to spare the poor lady's fame?"

"Indeed, sir, I have kept nothing back."

"And yet the story is marvellous strange as ye tell it, for ye had a gold chain with a jewel when the lady visited ye, and when she was gone the chain and jewel were gone also. If she had a mind to ye, not all the bolts and bars in Scotland would keep yon besom out. Now, I charge ye, tell me, Captain Andrew, not as sinner to confessor, but as a subject to his prince— was there no kindness between ye, no sort of dalliance, during which she might have shifted the gear from off your neck? No? Weel, ye maun back to Ruthven Castle as fast as ye may. Haste, man; away! away!"

But I saw not my way to Ruthven so plain. For whether the jewel were taken from me by human or devilish means I was equally at a loss to know who had it. And if I knew the thief, who could doubt that he had removed his prize to a place of safety? Then, to put myself again in the power of the Earl of Arran would be suicide—for now that other means had failed, he would not spare me. Methought his Highness was a trifle indifferent.

"Surely," said I, "I might serve your Majesty better outside the Castle of Ruthven than inside, where I should have half a dozen dirks in my puddings before I could pull off my boots."

"If it's danger you fear, Scotland is no place for you, for no part of it is safe for you or anybody else. The maist dangerous spot of all is this garden, and the man maist in danger is your anointed King. Why, man, there's a plot once a week, either to rive the liver forth of us, or to ravish our person from the realm. Ye are in greater danger here than anywhere else. But mark this—I have made it plain ere this to my Lord of Arran that I will not have his ward married until the jewels abstracted from our keeping are all returned to us. I could not deal mair openly with him, for I think not to name this X Jewel to him. Though men think otherwise, there are many things of State of which my Chancellor knoweth nothing; and, by the body of God! Captain Andrew, if this X Jewel be not returned to us, our Chancellor—braw lad as he is—may hang for a' we care. Ye see, we have given him a strong bribe to return it, for he is greatly set upon the marriage of this ward. And as for the lassie Uchiltrie, our wish is that ye should sift her thoroughly on this matter, for our mind misgives us that this is no devil's work, but some mischief of women."

"That is like enough, sir; but there are those

who have a shrewd guess of my errand, and the
gentle hand will not find this jewel. I could not
go back as I came without deserving and finding
the reward of a spy. But if the means could
be spared to give me some manner of warrant—"

"Sairts! would ye requisition us as ye would
the burgomaster of any mean Flemish town?
Ye call for our signature as ye would for a cup
of ale—the King's blank; the like was never
heard. And yet the matter presses. Maybe
Patrick hath not paid ower the taxes of his
sheriffdom of Forfar, as we required him, to the
chiel Hunter our glasingwright. But ye are better without the men; they would but lead ye
into temptation. Come into the lodging, and we
will find some better way for ye. The walls are
low, and wha kens how mony night-walkers
might spring in upon us at any moment."

So we went in, and the King wrote out and
handed to me a commission giving me absolute
control over the Castle of Ruthven and everybody within it. I thought that would serve at a
pinch, though I knew that my Lord of Arran
would not regard it. His Highness gave me,
moreover, a letter, couched in kindly terms, to
the Laird of Duncrub, requiring him to furnish
me with four fully equipped men for sixteen

days, in return for which service he offered his gracious thanks.

Thereupon I asked his Highness whether I was at liberty to seek his presence when he returned to Edinburgh. "If your horse will let you," said the King; "but dinna be flashing the bit paper in every carle's face. And we would have you carry this with you, so that, if at any time you get knowledge of the gear we were speaking of, you may return it to us. By which token we shall know that we may be easy upon the matter." Thereupon he gave me a topaz and dismissed me, in a homely manner patting me upon the check, and saying that I was a braw man.

As I might have expected, if I had had time to think of it, my dark friend was waiting for me at the door of the King's lodging, very anxious for an immediate conclusion with me. The night, however, was black as pitch, and, as I told him, the light, though good for murder, was very bad for fighting. The remark was not well received; but after some parley a rendezvous was arranged for six hours on the following morning by the windmill. This was no sooner agreed upon than from an upper window of the lodging came a voice, well-known to all, which said :

"Saul! but we will be there with the best of ye, and if we spy the Laird of Gautrie, we will hang him to the sail of the windmill before he can say his prayers."

So I was rid of a fool for that night; but I had reason to be sorry afterwards that I did not meet him by the windmill, for the townspeople of St. Andrews, who are a roystering crew, would have been present in great numbers, and a public lesson might have encouraged other men to be less pressing in their attentions to me.

Thinking that now I might go without further hinderance to my lodging, I started for the gate of the enclosure, my men carrying torches to show the way; but before I had gone many steps I was drawn aside by one whose figure I did not recognize in the gloom, but whose voice I well knew.

"Are you mad, friend Andrew," said this person, "that you would pass at this time of night, with lighted torches and only two attendants, through the streets of St. Andrews? Has the sight of your native Prince addled your wits?"

"Why," protested I, "it is but a few hundreds of yards to go. Besides, I have only been four hours in the town, and nobody outside this enclosure either knows or cares about me or my business."

8

"But they care about it inside the enclosure, and that is the serious matter for you. It is high time you knew Captain James a little better. He may not know your business, but he suspects it; and he is apt to treat a man he suspects as one he knows to be an enemy. As you well know, he has already made two indirect attempts upon your life. Did you not suppose that there were those here who knew you were coming, and waited to see the result of your interview with his Highness? Owing to some blunder—which I do not understand—about the letters you carried, you have, against their expectation, come out of the royal presence with a whole skin and a topaz in your pouch. Do you suppose, then, that you would ever come alive at your lodging with your torches and your two men?"

"But I can't mend matters," I interposed; "I cannot do otherwise."

"You can do otherwise; but I wish you to understand your danger. I dare say you think that Graham tickled your shins with his rapier out of mere devilry. Nothing of the sort. He's a Papist, and very great with the King for the moment; otherwise he would not have ventured to quarrel with you in the precincts of the Court. He is also very great with Captain James, who has broken for the present at least with the Min-

isters and the English Protestants. What is to
be the upshot of these intrigues no man can tell;
but sure am I that our master hath little liking
for the Man of Sin, and will have no serious dealings with him in the end if he can make his mar-
ket elsewhere. But in the meantime he is constrained to keep him in play."

"Master, I like not that. Do you make no re-
monstrance?"

"I go with the rest, in appearance. Man, I am
playing for my life, as you are for yours, though
you don't seem to know it. To be frank with
you, I have done with the Antichrist and his cup-
board of plate, and he shall go to perdition if I
can send him there. But to return to yourself,
Captain James means to be rid of you if he can,
and he is a man who has his eyes, ears, and hands
everywhere. He will strike whenever and wherever he can, so keep your wits a little more
alive. In the meantime bid your men put out
their torches and return by themselves to your
lodging by the Southgate. They will wait for
you at the foot of your stair, and I will give
you directions for your own return by another
route."

My men were therefore despatched by themselves, while the Master conducted me to a postern in the northern wall of the enclosure. One

of his men was waiting for us there, under whose guidance I came out by the Shore Port, and turned up by the Fishergate, past the Castle, and so into Northgate.

CHAPTER X

It marvels me in what disdain a woman will hold the wit of man. She will thankfully use it when she is in straits, but at other times she holds the cheapest subterfuge good enough to puzzle his dull brain. And she will play the sorriest of tricks at his very nose, in the full confidence that he does not see them.

I know not why this should be but that women are intoxicated by the power God hath given them over us. For some purpose they are permitted to work much evil by nature of their beauty and gentle manners. And such is not the philosophy of weak men only, for *mulier confusio hominis* was a saying well understood of Mr. Knox; and Mr. James Melvill, who, though sour enough in his Church politics, had some elements of humanity in his private life, hath told me that he trembled to think how far he was moved by fascinating women.

And I am fain to believe that women put down to their wit a good deal that is due to their beauty. Here had I been robbed of a gold chain by one of two women, but so great a contempt had the thief for my understanding that she left in my hands a clew to her identity in the shape of a collar of calcedonies. She had some reason for this; but I think not she knew she was preparing means for her detection, for women look not forward. There is much talk of their skill in practices and intrigue, but I respect not their plots. They are wondrous cunning and adroit, and when advised by men will do wonders. But their plots are full of windows, through which any one may look who will; and they are apt to believe that, if they shut their own eyes, no one else can see what they are doing.

But in this matter there was much I could not understand. If the Countess had the chain, why these attempts upon my life? Why did she not restore the jewel to the King and claim the marriage of her husband's ward? Was the jewel worth more than the right to dispose of a rich heiress in marriage? As for Jean Uchiltrie, I could conceive no motive strong enough to account for her being the thief.

I had, however, something more pressing to think of as I mounted my horse the morning following my interview with the King. I had to get back to Ruthven Castle, and the events of

the previous day told me that this might be a
difficult matter. Although at first strongly
moved not to return, I had changed my mind
upon that head. I was piqued by the loss of the
jewel, and, strange as it may seem, I had come
to think that my life would be nowhere so safe
as in Ruthven Castle. My reason for thinking
so I shall not here set down, because it is not
always well to lay bare the whole mind of a man,
and provoke idle charges of vanity and conceit.

Fully alive was I now to the danger of this
journey, and I had carefully considered the question of routes. The shortest road was through
Cupar and Lindores, or I might follow the shore
of the Tay, if I pleased, as far as Abernethy.
Again, by making a détour to the south, I might
ride as far as Strathmiglo, and, turning then at
right angles, reach Perth by the Pass of Dron.
But I rejected each of these routes, and determined to go by Glendevon and Gleneagles,
making a circuit so wide that nobody would
suspect me of entertaining it. So it was by
the Southgate Port that we rode out St. Andrews at six hours in the morning, intending to
avoid Cupar and reach the How of Fife by the
by-roads. But we had gone but a short distance
when a cry arose behind us, and, looking back,
we saw one running towards us.

This man had been charged to carry a letter to me before I started, but having missed me at my lodging had followed me to the gate. The letter, which came from a sure hand, contained the following passage:

"There are twelve men in the wood below the Hill of Moonzie, there are six at Ballinbreich on the low road by the Tay, and six in the Pass of Dron. Judge for yourself whether your best way is not by Glendevon. The enclosure came for you by my Lady Arran's post late last night."

This only gave me more serious reasons for the route I had already chosen, but the enclosure quite altered my mind. It ran thus:

"MONSIEUR LE CAPITAINE,—Ne revenez pas, je vous prie, sous prétexte aucun par le Glendevon, si vous tenez à la vie,   ELIZABETH."

What could this mean? The signature was royal in manner—or had it another meaning? But how knew the woman to speak of Glendevon, a route which of all others was the least probable for one coming from St. Andrews to take or even to think of? Was it that she knew the gate was beset for me on all the other routes? That was scarce probable. If not, was the warning meant in good faith? Unhappily, it was a question whether this woman ever did anything in good faith; and again she was not likely to trump her own cards; and yet—

The mention, however, of Glendevon was enough; the experiment was hopeless. Calling David Carryg to me at once, I said:

"David, you will take John Sloan and my horse and Barabbas. You will keep the south side of the hills until you strike the road which crosses to Dunning. You will follow that road into Strathearn, and on your way you will leave this letter with the Laird of Duncrub. The letter is in his Majesty's own handwriting, so that if any stop you a sight of the outside will reduce them to civility. That is all, except that you will wait for me at Ruthven Castle until I come."

Then, dismounting, I put the bridle into his hand, and would have bade the party godspeed, but that I saw Barabbas climbing deliberately from his saddle.

"Sir," said he, in a dogged manner, "I will be of your company."

"You will obey my orders, sir," retorted I: "you are not now in Ruthven Castle, and you will accompany my men wherever they go."

"I am sorry, sir; I must go with you whatever befalls. I dare not disobey my master's orders in this."

For a moment I was moved to end this difficulty in an obvious manner. My life was in danger, and this man's obstinacy threatened to put me to the extremity. I had a right to his life. Seizing one of my pistols, I balanced it for a moment in my hand; but catching sight of the face of the poor wretch, who made no movement to escape or protect himself, I dropped my hand. It is hard to strike a creature which does not resist. Moreover, the suspicion that he had perhaps done me some service with the papers which were crumpled into my gauntlet came back to me, and I relented.

"Well," said I, "if you must be an obstinate fool, you shall come with me; but listen carefully to the condition. For the next twenty-four hours you will neither leave my sight nor open your lips. You will be absolutely dumb, notwithstanding any temptation to speak which may be offered to you. If you say so much as 'Bobo Finla' I will put a bullet through your brain on the moment. Is that understood? Well, give your horse to Sloan; they can hire some rascals to help them by the way."

Thereupon, turning back towards St. Andrews,

I started him off at a very sharp pace along the path by the Common Lade, as they call the water which runs outside the southern wall of the city. When we had compassed one-half of the circuit of the place, by skirting the outside of this wall we came to the Haven, which faces to the north. And this we did in no great space of time, because, although the number of the inhabitants is great, their buildings do not cover much ground.

What I was purposed to do I had had in my mind before; so that I knew in what quarter to apply, and had no difficulty in finding a skipper to carry me to Dundee. It was an ill chance that the water was low at the time, and would not grow again for two hours so as to let us put out; for the Haven, which is fashioned by means of a wooden framework with stones inside, is much impaired by sand and rocks, and it is only at certain conditions of the tide that ships can enter or go out. The boat, moreover, in which we were to sail had no deck. Nevertheless, I caused Barabbas to embark with me, and, spreading the sail over the stern, we lay down beneath it, so as to escape the eyes of the curious and wait for the rising of the water.

I think I have seldom spent two hours so wholly miserable; but the tide came at last, and with it the skipper. Now it chanced that this skipper, having the half of our passage-money paid in advance, had so misused the two hours of waiting that he was plainly very drunk and blasphemous in his speech. But by the time I could creep out with safety and sit upright in the boat he was so far gone that he lay grunting in the bilge, out of all sense or knowledge. He was soon joined in that refuge by Barabbas, who, not being accustomed to go upon the sea, was seized with a sore sickness when we came into the rough water at the mouth of the Tay.

This might have been a serious matter if I had depended only on the skill of the skipper, for I was minded to land not at Dundee, but St. Johnston, and the Tay has so many sand-banks that none but an experienced mariner can sail a boat up it. It chanced, however, that there was a smart man on board who knew the river as well as the skipper; and I was glad that things fell out as they did, for I had less difficulty in persuading the younger man to take me up the Tay than I might have had with the skipper. But on no consideration would he consent to go as far as Perth, for the Pest was very hot there, and I had to be content to be landed by Elcho Castle.

When we were off Dundee the breeze died away, and we had to fall to the oars. This was indeed a severe labor, for the boat was heavy and the oars ill-made; but the lad and I worked with a will, so that for some days after I had little use of my sword-hand. I have scarce ever seen anything so beautiful as the country on both sides of this river, and I would fain have lingered on the journey but for my anxieties. When we had worked some distance up the river the course we were constrained to take brought us close under the walls of Ballinbreich Castle and past the landing-place of Newburgh. And here I grew anxious lest the horsemen set to intercept me at this point should spy me in the boat. But inasmuch as we could make no progress unless I took an oar, and I was afraid that my dress might draw the attention of those on the shore, I stripped myself naked to the waist, and so continued to row until we were out of the range of prying eyes.

At Elcho Castle, a few miles below St. Johnston, we took the land, and parted from the boatmen, Barabbas, who had recovered his stomach, lending a sly kick to the still recumbent skipper. From this point it was but a few miles inland to our destination, and I counted upon reaching it without difficulty by avoiding the beaten tracks and keeping to the rough ground.

It behooved us, however, to cross the King's

road from Falkland to Perth. As we came down the brae towards this road, the twigs crackling beneath our feet, Barabbas sought to stay me by catching at my cloak; but having my senses alive to other things, and forgetting for the moment that he was dumb, I cast him off impatiently. In a few seconds we were crossing the road; but we had hardly stepped upon it when a gentleman, followed by four other horsemen, rode out of a clump of trees and called upon us to stop.

"I am," said he, in a kindly manner, "the Sheriff of this county, or, rather, the Sheriff-Deputy, and I believe I have the good chance to speak to Captain Andrew Eviot."

"That is so, Mr. Sheriff," I replied; "can I serve you in any way?"

"The fact is," said he, in an embarrassed manner, "I am sorry to tell you that I hold a commission for your arrest for stealing a letter with violence from a rider named Joshua Henderson by the Clochrigstane."

Whereupon I laughed, saying, "If that is all, it is soon settled, for there is no truth in it, as I can easily prove." But I glanced with some suspicion at the companion of my voyage.

"That may well be," said the Sheriff; " but," he added, meaningly, "there's many a man thrown into jail on a trifling charge, and once he is in more dangerous matter is pretended against him. I hope it will not be so in your case. I am also charged to arrest one Carryg, your servant. I suppose this is he, although he hardly answers the description given me. Ho! you, sir; are you Carryg?"

To this Barabbas replied nothing, but shook his head; and being many times called upon, and giving no answer, he was about to receive some chastisement at the hands of the Sheriff when I thought right to interpose. At first I was more than content to watch his embarrassment; but seeing clearly that this was not a play prepared for my benefit, I explained that he was a servitor of my Lord of Arran, and was well known at Ruthven Castle. Whereupon Mr. Sheriff opened his eyes very wide, and seemed to be shrewdly puzzled; but some of his own men being acquainted with the appearance of Barabbas, which was singular enough, he was satisfied to discharge him.

Now the Tolbooth of Perth, whither I was constrained to go with the Sheriff, was an institution conducted on hospitable principles. My arms, it is true, were taken from me and hung up in the jailer's lodge; but in common with the other guests I was allowed to roam unchecked over the rest of the building, and there was no restriction as to food, provided a prisoner could pay for it. The jailer was devoted to his charges, and loved them more than the Bailies of Perth, who found him his wages. The Sheriff himself paid us a visit in the evening, with the special object of cheering his cousin, the Laird of Strowie, who was in jail for debt. Moreover, before leaving us he consumed two pints of ale and a chopin of auld wine, and smoked two pipes of tobacco, to his own great contentment.

The Laird of Strowie shook his head when he heard how I came to be cast into the Tolbooth.

"Sir," said he, "I was thrown in here six months ago for debt, though the whole country knows that I owe not a gray groat to any man. But it was in my Lady Jezabel's knowledge that I had been in the Raid of Ruthven, and she keepeth me here in the hope of wringing a large sum of money from me in purchase of my freedom. It is like that she looketh for the same from you."

I lay here some days in no discomfort of body, but in sore distress of mind. But on a certain morning, being Sunday, our jailer left the Tolbooth and its occupants to themselves. Whether the unusual sum I had given him by way of gratuity drew him to some congenial haunt, or he attended the morning preaching, about which the Ministers were now very noisy, I know not. But I took the opportunity of his absence to examine the only part of the building with which the guests were, as a rule, expected not to trifle. And when my companions saw what I was about they watched my motions with some interest.

The door of the Tolbooth was generally secured on the outside by a catband, but on this occasion the jailer had not put it on. Besides the catband there was a lock with a double and a single cast. What might have happened if the door had been locked with the double cast I cannot say, but in truth it was, on this as on many other mornings, locked only with the single cast. I soon found that my predecessors in the Tolbooth had, as was only natural, paid a good deal of attention to this lock; for not only was a large portion of the stone, into which the bolt was shot, broken away, but the bolt itself was half worn through with the frequent filings it had undergone. I had therefore nothing to do but insert my finger in the cleft of the stone and draw back the bolt, and the door of the Tolbooth stood wide open for those to go out thereat who would.

Taking down my sword, dagger, and pistols

from the wall in the jailer's lodge, I stepped out into the street, followed by the rest of the prisoners, who within an incredibly short time melted away and were seen no more. There was no one to stop us; the place was like a city of the dead. Whether this was due to the fear inspired by the Plague of Pestilence I cannot say, but at this time a citizen could scarce walk upon the street or the shore during the time of the preaching without being haled before the kirk-session, and maybe we of the Tolbooth owed more to the ministry of Perth than we wot of.

This exodus of its inhabitants from the Tolbooth without leave led to a prolonged lawsuit between the Bailies of Perth and an infuriate suitor whose debtor escaped with me. At several seasons, when much outcry has been made in the matter, the Bailies came very near to repairing the lock; but it is there as it was to this day, after a lapse of more than twenty years.

CHAPTER XI

In less than an hour I was mounting the steps leading to the apartments in Ruthven Castle occupied by my Lady Arran. In the room on the first floor I found two young men lolling on the seats in the window and pondering upon their dinner. To the elder of the two, who was wielding a picktooth, I addressed myself.

"Sir," said I, "if my Lady Arran is still at the castle, I shall be obliged if you will cause her to be informed that Captain Eviot seeks an interview with her."

The young gentleman looked at me, said nothing, and resumed the occupation of picking his teeth, which I had inconsiderately interrupted.

"I asked you a question, sir," said I, "which you appear not to have understood."

"My Lady will not see you," he replied, carelessly, and speaking with his back half turned upon me.

"Pray be good enough to take my message, and bring me my Lady's answer."

"Not I."

"Well, if you will not do your duty, I must make you do it," and, seizing him by the collar, I dragged him to the corner of the room, where, throwing back the tapestry, I entered upon the stairs leading to the upper floor. Up those steps I dragged him, taking care to permit his knees and other projecting members of his body to make acquaintance with the steps, which were of hard whinstone.

When we arrived at the upper floor he was the richer by a good many contusions, while his dress was disordered, and here and there frayed by contact with stone edges. This was not done without some noise, which brought out Mistress Kennedy, the Countess's gentlewoman.

"What meaneth this?" cried she.

"It meaneth, fair mistress, that this young gentleman refused to carry my name to my Lady, and that I have merely compelled him to show me the way up-stairs."

"And you have done well, sir. Of a truth my Lady will be glad to see you; but as for you, John Munro, if your impertinence comes to the ears of my Lady, you will have an ill time. You are a forward, lazy, conceited, useless varlet, and we should be well quit of you."

On my entry to the chamber my Lady appeared to be taken by surprise, but she greeted me with some warmth, taking both of my hands in hers. I cared not whether this cordiality was real or assumed. For the moment it allowed me to think that I was safe in Ruthven Castle. Mistress Jean, on the other hand, met me as one who had no interest in my coming.

"I am fortunate," said I—"fortunate in coming safely back, and in finding both of you fair ladies still here."

"I care not, as a rule," answered my Lady, "for a country life, but I have taken a strange fancy to this place. My Lord has unpleasant associations with it and likes it not. But Jean agrees with me that there is an air of romance about it. Is it not so, Jean?"

"I see nothing in the place," said Jean; "the society of M'Kuskan Grossok and Cristine does not go very far."

"You see, Captain Andrew, you and I count for nothing," remarked my Lady, with malice.

"Nay," retorted Jean, "my Lady is always engrossing, and Captain Andrew is really very funny."

There was clearly something amiss between the two. The Countess covered this retort by turning to me, and asking whether I had met my Lord on my way.

"I could hardly do that," said I, "unless my Lord took ship at Perth, for I came by boat to the Castle of Elcho, and should have been here some nights ago but that I was thrown into the Tolbooth at Perth on a charge of stealing a letter." Whereat my Lady was greatly surprised, and showed signs of displeasure.

"Who did this? And if it were so, how came you hither?"

"I simply walked out at the front door of the Tolbooth, and here I am. As for my accuser, he was one of my Lord's men named Henderson; but I need hardly say there was no truth in the charge."

"He shall hear more of this, I pledge my word. But, in truth, we are rather dull here, Captain Andrew, and wish to be amused. Have you had any other good-fortunes?"

"Well, to say sooth, I have. I found a chain." I noticed that Jean's eyes were fixed on the ground.

"You are rather fond of chains, are you not?"

"I have not had much experience in them. The only other chain I ever had in my possession was stolen from me" (Jean was clearly displeased); "but I will show you that which I found, for one of you two ladies may have lost it." And I produced the chain of calcedonies from my doublet.

"It probably belongs to some serving-woman," said my Lady, eying it indulgently. But before I could look at Jean Uchiltrie she had snatched it from my hand, crying, with great indignation: "How dare you, sir? That is mine; where did you get it? Did you bribe somebody to steal it from me?" And without further words she flung out of the apartment.

"What in the name of John Knox does that mean?" said I, my eyes wide open with astonishment.

"Ah!" laughed my Lady, softly, "men never do understand us; but of all the stupid men I ever saw you are the most stupid. Why, man, can you not see that the girl is in love with you, and meant you to keep the chain as a gage? Then you bring it here, and before another of her own sex make a jest of it. I wonder she did not tear your eyes out. But you are right to treat it lightly; I have had great trouble with her, and her fancy will change to some other man in a month. But tell me where you 'found' this chain."

"Nay," said I, "I have already said too much about it; I will say no more." And I had my own opinion of my Lady's surmise, and my stupidity, and Mistress Jean's fanciful nature. I was not so stupid as I looked.

"Well, we will drop that subject; but tell me, did you get a letter from me about Glendevon? Well, Andrew, you believe that I am your friend?" And she spoke softly, coming close to me and putting her hand upon my arm; and—well, she was assuredly a very handsome woman, but I lost not my head.

"Have I not the best reason to know my Lady for my friend?"

"Well," continued she, "if you know that, you know that there are two sides to friendship. I would have you help me as I help you. You have interested me, and I will make your fortune if you will be a friend to me. I want your help."

"I know of no way in which so humble a person as I can serve you; but if you will make your meaning plain, I will try."

"I think you understand my meaning; but in case you don't, I will ask you a plain question: Have you ever heard of the X Jewel?"

"Yes," said I, "I have heard of it; it is said to be a Papist jewel."

"Where did you hear that?" she asked, sharply, with the manner of one who had me in a trap.

"Mr. Andrew Melvill said so on Monday night in St. Andrews."

"How dare you jest with me, sir?" she cried, in great anger. "The whole world knows that Mr. Andrew fled to England many months ago, and dares not show his nose in St. Andrews."

"So my Lord told me," replied I, with a great calm, "the last time I was here. The whole world knows it; but the whole world does not know that Mr. Andrew was in St. Andrews on Monday last."

"Did you see him, sir?"

"Nay, but I heard him. I may as well tell you the whole story, as it is known to all the horse-boys and grooms who follow the Court. His Highness and Mr. Andrew were disputing in a chamber with an open window last Monday night, and Mr. Andrew charges his Highness with carrying the X Jewel, being the mark of the Beast, in his bosom; whereupon his Highness declares *in verbo Principis*, that, if such a thing exists, he knows not in what part of the world it is."

"Is that all?" said my Lady, relapsing into her ordinary humor. "Perhaps there is no such thing. And yet," she added, as if speaking to herself, "he is fond of a grim jest."

"What is the jest?" said I.

"Jest? Did I say jest? Oh! there is no jest in it." But I said to myself that I knew what she meant. The King was fond of a practical joke at the expense of the members of his Court, and he was quite capable of making one of them miserable about the supposed loss of a jewel, while he was actually carrying it suspended about his neck. Such a trick he was capable of playing upon my Lord and Lady of Arran, but I knew he would not play it upon me. This doubt in my Lady's mind, and her evident earnestness about the whole matter, set my mind at rest upon one point. Whoever had the jewel, she had it not.

"I doubt," continued the Countess, "whether there is such a jewel; but it truly is said that a jewel belonging to the King is missing, and I have thought that this girl may have taken it. She had the opportunity—that much is certain. She is a strange, secretive creature, and I can make nothing of her. My Lord, as I dare say you know, has the gift of her marriage, and it may be that she resents this; but, believe me, she has given me much anxiety. She seems to have a liking for you; and you can help me in this—you can tell me what you think of her."

This was in effect what I desired, and I could not pass the chance. I wished to have the opportunity of speaking to Mistress Jean; but neither to the King nor to this woman did I engage to betray her secrets if she confided in me, nor indeed did any such idea enter into my mind. So I replied, temperately, to my Lady:

"If it is your wish to know what I think of this young lady, you must give me the chance of speaking with her — a chance I have as yet not had."

"You shall certainly have every possible opportunity." And indeed my Lady was as good as her word, for I was constantly in the company of both of these ladies; and the Countess from time to time, as she had the chance of doing so without appearance of intention, left me alone with Mistress Jean, but always in the garden, a good view of which could be got from the house. But the plot entirely missed its mark, for no sooner was I alone with the girl than, as if she knew what passed between myself and my Lady, she became silent and morose, and refused to speak with me. And this continuing for some space, both my Lady and I began to be very far from content.

CHAPTER XII

THIS was a state of things which could not last. For a time my Lady was very great with me, treating me on terms of familiarity and friendship. But erelong I fancied that she began to fall out of conceit with me. Whether she thought me useless, or maybe her enemy, it was enough that I seemed to have failed her. I doubt not that, if I had been able to run their course, this woman and my Lord of Arran would have proved as faithful friends as most other Court politicians in Scotland, or, for that matter, in any other country in the world. But I had my own course to run, and though I lived on terms of intimacy with my Lady and her ward, the intimacy stopped at a certain point. Like all imperious and selfish women, she was vain, and though she may have had little real value for me, she could not endure that I should prefer the younger woman to her. And I fear she came to feel this—for it is a thing women quickly detect or men easily betray—although I endeavored to conceal it, and Mistress Jean avoided me like poison. So it came about that my Lady would leave the castle for periods of two or three days at a time, for she had much business on hand, and Ruthven began to lose its romance in her eyes.

I was at that time riding a great black horse with a white spot on its forehead and three white feet. It was a beautiful creature, and as generous in its temper as its appearance. It chanced one morning that, when he was brought out of his stable by John Sloan, my Lady and Mistress Jean were present; and, as some women are prone to do, Mistress Jean showed him much courtesy, stroking his sleek coat, caressing, and even talking to him. All which the good beast, who was accustomed to kind treatment—for he was a horse which even the devil himself would not ill use—seemed to understand, and accepted with pleasure.

"By what name call you this horse, Captain Andrew?" said the girl.

"I call him Black Ouviot, which is a good name for a good horse."

"Nay, I think not that that is his name—is it, old fellow? But where got you him?"

"I think I shall not tell you, Mistress Jean. I begin to think you would claim him from me, and as he is worth his weight in gold to me, I cannot give him up."

This was no vain protest, for the theft of horses was as fruitful a source of quarrels and feuds in Scotland as the disposing of teind sheaves. Men were hanged or drowned every day "for" horses, staigs, or mares, as well as for humbler and less useful creatures. It was the habit of the thief to sell the stolen horse as promptly as possible, and therefore often at a low price. But whether the new owner acquired him fairly or not, he was loath to give him up. Mr. George Buchanan, for all that he was a great scholar, was "extreme vengeable against any that offendit him," and did much mischief to my Lord of Morton for a hackney which my Lord bought after it had been stolen from Mr. George. Indeed, but for Mr. George's allowance of it, the practice against the Regent might never have taken a beginning. And all for a horse!

Mistress Jean's question was simple enough, and it was simply put; no stranger would have thought it anything but idle. I could see what my Lady thought of the episode, but my Lady did not understand this girl, and she was wrong. I, however, knew that the question had something behind it, because relations were so strained between Mistress Jean and myself that she would not willingly have shown interest in anything belonging to me. And I mention it because, as will be seen, there was something behind it.

The day following this question about my horse, one Berald Stewart, a cousin of my Lord of Arran, came to seek an interview with my Lady. With him were two other gentlemen, one of whom was said to be a son of the Laird of Graden, who looked as if he feared the face of no man, but went where and did whatsoever he listed. But for all his bold countenance, the man was simple in his manner and free from arrogance; and I told myself that, if I had not remembered awry all that I had heard, this man was not a son of Graden, but my Lord of Bothwell.

The demeanor of Berald Stewart I liked not, and as I was not yet prepared for an open rupture with my Lady and her friends, I troubled her guests with but little of my presence. But I noted with admiration the arrogance of her bearing to them as compared with her kindness to me, and I misliked it. By-and-by, however, this Berald Stewart, accompanied by my Lord of Bothwell, coming down the steps from the first floor, sought me in the garden.

"Ha," said the former, "the chain-finder!"

"What mean you, feather-head?" replied my
Lord.

"The poor devil of a capitaine, who finds chains
for ladies."

"I would he might find a chain for thy fool's
tongue, thou addle-pated chatterbox. If it be
yonder man you speak of, by God's death! he
looketh to me to be the man to do it."

"Francis, Francis, you know that I love you,
and will take all your hard words without offence; but you are in the wrong about this man
of chains."

"Hout, hout, ye bear with my words because
ye darena refuse them. But what the devil have
ye to do with this gentleman? If ye provoke
him, he will cut your comb for ye, for I trow he
is the better man. Believe me, Berald Stewart,
ye are no match for that man. I have an eye
for such matters."

"I will show you that your eye deceives you at
times. Ah! my captain, how is the weather for
chains?" This he addressed in a loud voice to me.

"It seems," replied I, "good enough weather
for chaining your tongue to your lugs. I am
somewhat of my Lord's opinion about you."

"Ah!" said my Lord, "is it so; do ye know
me, man? To be sure there's more know Francis
Stewart than Francis Stewart knows."

"Be assured, my Lord; my tongue is not, like your friend's, in need of chaining. If I know you, I will keep my own counsel."

Hereupon Berald Stewart got his word in again.

"Who's tongue, sir, were you good enough to say you would chain?"

"I would," retorted I, with some irritation, "that thou wert chained by the tongue to the fork at the end of the devil's tail, and that he would drag thee—"

"Would you? I suppose you are prepared to give me the satisfaction I have a right to ask for this—at once?"

"Surely, at once."

"With one or two persons present to see that all things are done in order?"

"With everybody present who is within hail of the castle, and cares to attend." And calling aloud for Carryg, I bade him warn all the men who were about to attend within five minutes in the Watery Meadow. This meadow lay between two thickets outside the garden wall. The garden itself would have been the better place, but we could scarce desecrate with our combat the retreat of the ladies in the castle.

Within but a short space of time about forty or fifty persons, being gentlemen, gentle-

10

men's gentlemen, servants, husbandmen, and jackmen, stood round a small open space in the Watery Meadow, in the midst of which Berald Stewart was to have his satisfaction. When we had removed our doublets, the sun having passed the meridian by two hours, we drew lots for the western position, and the lot falling to me, we took our places and engaged at once.

I soon found that this man had more sense in his sword than his tongue. So far as science went, I knew all that the Italian fencers of the day practised, but this man also knew it. And being master of his science, he went somewhat beyond it, and did what some masters of fence were tempted to do. From time to time he would indulge in combinations which were in defiance of all the known rules. This method is likely to be very deadly with those who, though knowing the rules, are not complete masters of them. To a man like myself, to whom the practice of those rules was a second nature, these outbursts were not so embarrassing, but they were very dangerous to the man who practised them.

In particular he made use of a certain curved thrust, which was very dangerous to him in this sense, that its use must of necessity leave his guard open for a moment. The first time he tried it he touched me slightly on the outside of

the arm, and the cut, though slight, bled profusely. The second time I only saved it with the
counter-guard of my sword. The third time—
what happened the third time passed so quickly
(I might say it passed more quickly than thought)
that no description in words can give an accurate
idea of it. I speak now of things I noticed, or
things I thought; but they passed so quickly
that it seems more correct to say that I felt
them.

After my adversary had used this curved
thrust for the second time, I became conscious
that it was on both occasions preceded by a sort
of shiver in his arm. When I saw the shiver for
the third time, I simply ran him through the
body.

Speaking of the thing afterwards in cold blood,
I can only explain it by saying that I knew there
was a moment before the thrust came in which a
quick stroke might get past his guard. When I
saw the shiver I ran the risk of assuming that
the curved cut was coming again, and without
looking at his sword I ran him through on the
moment. My instinct was right.

"That shows," said my Lord Bothwell, as
Stewart's men were busied with him, "that a man
may be a good fencer and a bad fighter. This
poor devil had skill of fence, but no brains; and

so he must needs use that thrust three times with a swordsman who knew what to do with it."

Then he drew me a little apart and said :

"Captain Eviot, this matter has done me much good. I feel a better man after it, and I am not an over good one. But, my friend, this will come to the King's lugs, which are longer than they ought to be, as I know to my cost. He liketh not the sight of cold steel, nor those who use it. But I am your witness that the quarrel was none of your seeking; only I must be out of this country before you appeal to my testimony. Nay, I will do better, man; I will write to his Majesty. It is my painful duty to write often to my cousin James about his own miscarriages; and though he taketh my letters in but ill part, he knoweth that I do not bear false witness."

As I was wiping the blood from my sword with a wisp of grass, I caught sight of a pale face with glittering eyes on the outskirt of the crowd. It was Jean Uchiltrie.

CHAPTER XIII

THE little crowd was melting away and breaking into small clusters, discussing the encounter with deep interest. Now and then a man would break into gestures, making thrusts in pantomime to enforce his meaning, while others would shake their heads.

But what did Mistress Jean at such a meeting? Being minded that she should remain no longer on the ground, I passed to where she stood; but before I could speak her sharp eyes had seen what I myself had for the moment forgotten.

" You are hurt," she said, pointing to the blood which was still dripping from my arm.

" Nay, it is no more than a scratch; some scratches bleed freely. But what do you here? This is not a sight for your bright eyes to look upon."

" I could not help it. I saw from the tower what was passing, and I could not stay there and look on at a distance. I am glad I came."

" You must go now; you cannot be permitted to remain on such a scene."

" I will go, but I would say something first. I must speak with you. Can you be under the beech-tree in the garden just before dusk?"

" You may count on my being there, if it will serve you in any way."

Women are sadly out of place on such occasions, and I was glad to see her go, for Cristine, who had come with her, was on the point of going into hysterics.

Whether my antagonist yet lived I knew not. His people had carried him to the basement of the castle, and now I made my way to my own apartment, where Carryg bound up my arm. It was slashed, not dangerously, but so as to require some slight attention. And for some hours I lay on my pallet nursing it. Towards dusk I stole out and found my way to the beech-tree in the garden, and here I was joined before many minutes by Mistress Jean. It seems that at this hour it was my Lady's practice to shut herself up in an apartment where she consulted the occult powers as to the future, and Jean availed herself of the respite to escape from the house.

" Captain Eviot," said she, defiantly, " you will readily believe that only very strong mo-

tives would have made me seek this interview."

"I can have no difficulty in understanding
that," I replied, somewhat dryly. She was too
ready to show me that this meeting was not due
to any interest she took in me.

"What is a matter of life or death to me may
seem trifling to you."

"That is clearly impossible."

These curt replies annoyed her, as I meant
they should; for, though herself much given to
irony, in common with the rest of her sex she
could ill bear to be made the subject of it.

"It may be everything in the world to me,"
she continued, "and it will cost you nothing to
give it."

"Very well, Mistress Jean; to come to the
point, what is it?"

"I would have you tell me where you got
your horse." I opened my eyes in some astonishment, and marvelled what this might mean.
After some thought I answered her thus:

"Mistress Jean, some time since you asked me
a question about a ballad you heard me sing,
which I could not answer. And because I could
not answer, you called me a spy. Was that
well?"

"Surely I hope not."

"You hope not? And mean you that you ask a service of me—be it a trifle, if you will have it so—when you hope I am not a spy?"

"Nay, I do not think it. I did not think it then; I never thought it; I would I had never said it."

"Well, I could tell you now, if so you wish it, what you asked me then—it has come back to my remembrance. And surely I could tell you somewhat about Black Ouviot, though possibly not so much as you would wish to know. But whereas the jade Fortune has made of me a soldier, Nature meant me for a tradesman, and it is my rule never to do anything for nothing."

"Whatever I may think of others, I could scarce think that of you."

"You have thought much worse of me than that, to judge from the manner in which you have used me for some time back. For a friend, for one who trusts and believes in him, a man will do much. But be not mistaken; even an auld sang has its price in this world, or the story of a ballad and a horse."

"And what may your price be, sir? They tell me I am rich."

"Tell me," said I, wholly disregarding the sneer, "what you know about the jewel, and I will answer your question, and possibly as many more as you may be pleased to ask."

" I can tell you nothing," she replied in a low voice, and looking on the ground. She said not that she had knowledge of the jewel, but I thought she had.

" I thought you said this was a matter of life and death to you, and yet you will pass it by that you may keep your own knowledge of a miserable chain."

" I can tell you nothing," she repeated ; " but your miserable chain seems to be a matter of death and life to you."

" It is; but you women expect to get all things you ask for in this world and give nothing in return. The chain is as vital to me as the horse and ballad are to you."

" Ask me not ; I can tell you nothing." Her tone was despondent; then she roused herself and spoke with some passion :

" You are a man and strong; have you no pity for a weak and friendless woman? Have you no generosity in your strength that you can give me nothing without a return? I am alone in this place, held down by a hateful woman, without father or mother, without friends or kin to protect me; and when I ask you a question which concerns one who was dear to me above

all in this world, and which it would cost you
nothing to answer, you talk about your price.
If I had thought you a man of 'honor,' such as
many we have in this country, I should not have
asked you, but I thought not of you in that
way."

I know not why—for what was this girl to
me?—but when she spoke of one dear to her
above all others, my blood seemed to turn sour.
Read me this riddle if ye can, ye wise, for it
passed my understanding.

"When you speak," said I, "of one who was
dear to you, mean you him to whom my Lord of
Arran would marry you?"

"What! the man you killed this afternoon!
Assuredly not."

"That man! was he to be your husband? I
knew it not, but now I begin to understand. Nor
knew I that he was dead."

"I cannot hope he is not. As you might expect, they would marry me to a Stewart if they
could. But I had a right to expect that they
would at least choose a man for me, and not
a mean, selfish, conceited coxcomb. God be
thanked, there is a reservation in the gift of my
marriage, and they shall marry me only where
I please. But if you must know, I spoke not of
a lover or a husband, but of my father, who was

dearer to me than all other men. The ballad you sang is his ballad, and Black Ouviot was his horse."

At this I felt my courage begin somewhat to abate. But I asked myself—was this true? And if she believed it, might she not be mistaken? Had not all nations under the sun, whether Parthians, Medes, or Elamites, or the dwellers in Mesopotamia, in Pontus and Asia, long ago settled that men should give no credit to the tales of women? Well, I had heard many tales from men which were villanous lies, and I had known some women's tales which proved to be true, so that the rule of nations held not always. It was a hard thing to be churlish to this girl; for the mixture of entreaty and defiance in her was scarce not to be admired, and in truth she had touched me where I was most open to a wound. To yield would be to give up the weapon by which I hoped to win the jewel. But then to show myself a scurvy fellow—above all, to Jean Uchiltrie—there, it could not be done by me. And thrusting from me all thought of what I might lose by it, I said to myself I would surrender: but still it should be upon terms, for the mercantile instinct was strong within me.

"Think not, Mistress Jean," I said at length, "that you have not moved me. But you may be mistaken. Others have been known to sing that ballad, I trow, and one horse is sometimes not unlike another."

"The horse knew me."

"Well, so be it; it is like he did. I would fain barter with you still, but I cannot do it. You think it costs me nothing to tell you what you ask. It may cost me everything, and in sooth I think not I would do it for any other woman."

"Ah! was I not right—did I not know you? I have never indeed doubted you in my heart; never since—but I scarce can bear to see you laughing and jesting and plotting with the ogress who watches over me, and every hour of the day studies to wound and pain me."

"You know something, but you may not know that I carry my life in my hand in this castle; and, surely, if a man does no worse, he may laugh and jest with the devil in defence of his life. As to your questions, the horse I bought in the town of Berwick two days before I came hither. Buying it in Berwick, I know it must have come from Scotland, because while an Englishman will always sell a horse honestly come by to a Scot, from whom he gets a better price, yet he is not likely to sell in Berwick a horse stolen in England. The seller said that it came

to him from Cockburnspath, and I make no
doubt that it was stolen in Scotland and taken
across the English lines to be sold.

"As for the ballad, I must tell you that, before
landing at Berwick, I tried to land at the Fastcastle, and when half-way up the steps leading
to the keep I heard some one sing the verse you
asked about. Whose was the voice, or from
where it came, I could not tell. I like not to raise
hopes in your mind which may be disappointed,
but I may tell you that Cockburnspath is but a
few miles from Fastcastle. Of course, that may
be but a coincidence. But believe me, and I
speak in all seriousness, you can never find the
truth of this sad story until an end is made with
James Stewart, callit the Earl of Arran, and if
you could say anything about the chain—"

"I can tell you nothing," she said again, in a
low voice; "it may seem ungracious, but I cannot. If you knew you would know I cannot.
But you hold me grateful from my heart for all
time, and there is my hand in token thereof.
And now, fare thee well, Andrew Eviot, for we
shall be parted ere many days; but we shall
meet again, though not yet awhile. Well I know
we shall meet again. And if thou art ever in
sorrow or sickness, or poor and friendless, think
that there is one who will have thee always in

her thoughts, for thou hast had mercy on the fatherless."

She went before I could speak in answer, and —well, had I my reward?

There are many who, reading this, would say I chose the better part; or, seeing the like at the playhouse, would be the first to applaud. And yet these same, being perhaps of the most debauched, when they came to the practice of daily life, would flout me for a fool. And the world—it is a cold, hard world—would say of one who held to his own, without pity for the weak and helpless, and thereby gained distinction, that he was a wise and capable man; but of him who yielded that he was weak and threw away his chances, and was unfit for affairs.

But I know not. I who write this am a man of many sins and transgressions, for the remission of which I look, not to man, but to an all-merciful God. But I have ever hoped that, when the great book of Time is opened, there will be found written therein the few acts of kindness God has permitted me to do, to my own loss and prejudice. I look not that they should be counted for righteousness, but that it may be thought in mercy that I caught a few rays of light from the Great Example. For did not He, who had not where to lay His head, go about doing good?

There is one who has for his motto, " Thou shalt want ere I want," and who has risen to great place in these days. He pacified the Borders, besieging and burning men's homes over their heads without form or pretence of trial, and cutting down those who attempted to escape. I know not whether in all things he be true to his motto; but if so, he has need, in truth, to be a godly man in his walk and conversation.

CHAPTER XIV

I suppose all men have a soft place in them, although, like the spring of a secret drawer, it is not easily found. This girl had hit upon the soft place about me, and for some time after she had gone I could scarce recover my balance. I could see now how miserable and cheerless her life was rendered by those who professed to protect her; and, although she was styled an heiress, I knew too well that her property would be practically confiscated by the man whom they forced her to marry.

I could see also with some clearness the truth about her father's disappearance. He had been hurried, along with his horse, probably under cloud of night, across the water at the Queensferry, and before the sun rose again he was within the walls of Fastcastle. The place had an evil name, but only those who had an intimate acquaintance with it knew the story of its secret dungeons. There was, however, a cavern on the sea-level immediately below the keep, and it was generally believed that there were various cham-

bers in the rock which supplied a communication
between the cavern and the castle. It was possible that the song I heard came from one of
those chambers, and if so the impression made
on me of a voice coming from a distance was
explained. As for the horse, it was probably
stolen, or sent purposely for sale to Berwick, that
it might not give a clew to the fate of its former
master.

The coincidence was singularly striking, and
would have justified an appeal to any ordinary
monarch. But my native Prince had his irons
in many strange fires, and he who hit his minions ran the risk of striking the Prince himself.
George Uchiltrie, moreover, had got into trouble
about the secret hoards of the Regent Morton,
and the mere mention of a secret hoard kindled
the imagination of this King to such a degree
that he lost his common-sense, of which as a rule
he had no small share. On the other hand, though
he affected not women, he could not endure that
defenceless women should be harshly treated, and
this weakness in his nature was so strong that
many designing creatures took an unjust advantage of it.

As for myself, my position was critical and
my work but half done. My endeavors had
not been fruitless. I knew that my Lady had

11

not recovered the jewel; and while I felt certain that Jean Uchiltrie could tell me where it was, I was equally certain that she would not speak, and I had no clew to her motive. I was to leave the puzzle unsolved, for I could not now doubt that Berald Stewart's visit and insolence were meant as a declaration of war by my Lord and Lady Arran. His signal failure was likely to double their exasperation, for knowing his skill of fence they had not doubted that he would give a good account of me. And this is why I was sorry I had not met the Laird of Gautrie at St. Andrews, for if I had Berald Stewart had never visited Ruthven Castle. Clearly I must go from this sooner or later, only I was unwilling to be driven out of the place without some assurance that my danger was actual. So I despatched John Sloan that night to Falkland with a letter containing a full account of the affair with Berald Stewart. This letter was directed to one who was even better able than I to judge the meaning of these events, but I grudge to mention his name.

The following morning, as I was pondering these matters in the garden, my Lady came to me and said she would speak with me.

"Come hither," said she, "to yonder beech-tree, where we can talk freely." I had rather it

had been anywhere else. It seemed strange, and
I liked it not that I should be talking with this
woman on the spot where I spoke with Jean the
night before, but I could not mend it. Had she
chosen the place because she knew of my meeting with my Lord's ward?

"Andrew," she said, when we were under the
tree, "you have done a foolish thing."

"What have I done, madame?"

"How could you go and quarrel with Berald
Stewart?"

"My Lord of Bothwell—"

"Hush, hush! don't mention his name. None
knew that he was here. Above all, don't speak
of him to his Highness if you do not wish to in-
jure him." I took care not to tell her that my
Lord had probably written ere this to the King.

"My Lady," said I, "I had no choice in the
matter. Berald Stewart sought me out here,
and fastened a quarrel upon me which I could
not without disgrace avoid."

"I know, I know. He is a fool and you are
a man, and that's the whole of it. But you
might have kept out of the way. You know not
what I have done for you. His Highness took
you in suspicion when you came to Edinburgh,
and sent you here. That should have made you
more cautious. You well know that you have

enemies anxious to do an ill turn to a man who is unpopular at Court, and I have stood between you and them. But for me you would have had the Sheriff of the county here about that affair at the Tolbooth of Perth."

"He would have got a warm reception, I assure you."

"And then you do this thing, which will cause you endless trouble. The King has no sympathy with such folly, and I know not what more I can do for you."

I thought it wiser not to answer this. I would not tell her what she either did not, or pretended not, to know. And I knew not how much truth there was in what this strange woman said.

"Andrew," she continued, "I have always liked you—I don't like many people besides myself—and I thought I should have you always with us. But even with that wretched girl you have given me no help. If you have learned anything you have not told me."

This speech rather jarred upon me, for it implied that I had promised to act as a spy on Jean Uchiltrie, and, moreover, that I had kept my information to myself and been false to both sides. I determined to put this right at once.

"My Lady Arran," said I, "I think you misapprehend. I promised that, if you gave me the opportunity of judging, I would tell you what I thought of Mistress Jean, and I now tell you that I think her an honest, simple-minded girl. But as for the jewel you spoke of, though I took not in hand to report upon that matter, she has told me nothing, and that I can say without harm."

" Have you asked her about it?"

" I have."

" Have you mentioned the jewel by name to her?"

" I have."

" And what said she?"

" She said nothing, but made as if she understood me not."

" I mind it weel. It was round yon mulberry-bush that he came—I was but a bairn at the time—and said, ' Better bairns greet than bearded men.' The auld carle! I'm right glad he is not here now, nor like to be. Did ye say he would come back, man? God forbid! Na, na; the Maister of Glamis is weel enough where he is, and there he'll bide maybe until God be pleased to call us in succession to our dearest cousin of England, when he will have to seek other lodging; for there will be no coming back here in our time. The day of enterprises is over."

This speech came from behind the mulberry-bush which hid us from the speaker, and to my great relief put an end to my converse with my Lady. It was the custom of my master, the King—an innocent custom, but embarrassing to some of his subjects—to visit them in an unceremonious way without due warning. A messenger had, indeed, been sent on half an hour in advance; but as no one knew where the Countess was, the message had not been delivered to her. In addition to the numerous company which followed the King, many of the neighboring barons came to pay their respects to his Highness; and how food was found for them all I know not, but I suppose the escheat of my Lord of Gowrie bore the expense.

His Highness caught sight of my Lady and myself as we rounded the mulberry-bush to meet him. He was attired in a riding-coat of scarlet, he had a high crowned hat with a large feather on his head, and carried a hawk-glove on his hand.

"After sair searching, madame," he cried, "we have found ye; but although we took your castle by assault before ye knew we were at the gate, we see ye are not without protection. For all men ken that Captain Eviot is ready enough with his sword."

The cynicism of this speech was readily caught by those in attendance, and if I had not gathered it from the sober manner in which the King acknowledged my obeisance, the hard looks of those about him would have told me but plainly enough that I was supposed to be in disgrace. Of course it was the affair with Berald Stewart.

"But in sooth, madame," he continued, "we have come hither purposing to dine with you, partly for our pleasure and partly that we might converse with the loon Grossok, who, as we are informed, liveth in this castle and hath some knowledge of the abominable blasphemies which Sathan is permitted to put forth at this time in the kirk-yard of Glendevon."

A slight color came into my Lady's face at the mention of Grossok's name. And well it might, for Grossok could tell more of my Lady's dealings than was convenient, and there was no assurance of what he might say when under the King's influence. There is a certain toleration of witchcraft and divination in this country, but at times the Scots are carried away by a deluge of fanaticism, and persons of the highest rank (of whom my Lady Glamis is the example most notorious) are sent to the stake. In many cases it hath been observed that the persons put to death for witchcraft are obnoxious in regard of their political conduct, but to the victims it matters not whether they are executed for political reasons or for witchcraft.

"Grossok?" said my Lady. "Yes, indeed there is one named M'Kuskan Grossok, who is my secretary; but inasmuch as he is a most devout man, I should doubt his having any knowledge of those who deal with Sathan."

"Weel, weel, we trust not, but we would have speech with him presently. For the moment there is a gentleman here in whose ear we would say a word in season, and we would have the rest of ye interrupt us not until we have occasion to summon ye." So, beckoning to me, he led the way to the middle of the bowling-green, where, turning sharply round, he laid his hand familiarly upon my arm, a gesture which must have been well seen by those who witnessed the asperity of his manner to me a few moments before.

I thought, as doubtless the on-lookers also thought, that the affair with Berald Stewart was the subject of this word in my ear. But once out of ear-shot the King seemed to forget that he was within sight of his courtiers.

"Have ye come ony speed, man?" he said, eagerly.

" Does your Highness mean in respect of the jewel?"

" Aye, what else would I be speiring at ye for?—the bit Papist chain we spoke of when ye were at St. Andrews."

" Well, sir, I cannot tell you where it is, but I can tell you where it is not."

" That's always something; but mean you that yon besom of a Countess hasna got it?"

" That is what I mean."

" And how may you know that?"

" I know it from the woman's feverish anxiety to regain the jewel, and her attempts to bribe me to help her in getting it."

" That's a good telling, anyhow," said the King, his face brightening; " but say you that she spoke openly of it to you, calling it the X Jewel?"

" She did; but not knowing how far I was informed, threw doubts upon the character of the chain."

" Were ye discreet, man, to let on that ye had ever heard tell of the chain?"

" It was known at St. Andrews, sir, that Mr. Andrew Melvill had charged you with having the chain, and I thought well not to deny having heard something of the matter."

" That all comes of our good-nature, which is

ower good for some folk. But what of the lass, Captain Andrew? It is ill work guessing; but our experience, which is not small in such matters, tells us that, if the thief was not the aulder besom, it was the lassie Jean."

"So I thought, sir; but she will not speak. She claimed the chain of calcedonies, and I have told her that she put the jewel chain round my neck with her own hands; but to that, as well as to all else I said, she made as if she understood me not. Your Majesty may be able to move her, but sure am I that nobody else will."

"Weel," said the King, "we will have speech with her upon this matter after our dinner. But I am minded to mention to ye what I was near forgetting. They have made a stir to disgrace you, sir, in regard to your affair with Berald Stewart. We like not that pestilent French humor, and if ye had been to blame we should not have spared ye; but we know the whole truth of the matter, and are not sorry to know that there are some men yet in our kingdom. We had a letter from my Lord of Bothwell about ye, and though the poor body hath neither mind nor manners, he is an honest man in suchlike matters. So ye can be at rest upon that point."

The company the King brought with him was not only numerous, for it included most of the

men then in favor at the Court; and after they
had dined the quiet garden saw a gayer scene
than it was accustomed to. Men in varied colors of satin and silk walked over the grass or
stood in groups and talked. Their unusual number was shortly explained, for the elegant young
man I had seen in the King's Chamber at St. Andrews was good enough to make the matter plain
to me. But while he spoke his demeanor was
so light and careless that none without hearing
would have guessed what he was saying.

"Andrew," said he, "will you stand by me, if
need be?"

"I am bound to stand by you, whether in good
report or evil report."

"That is but what I thought. I got your letter, and, if I may say so, I think you may safely
stay here for a day or two, until you hear further from me; I can think of no other place
where the danger would not be greater. I am
told that they have made up their minds to stick
me in the King's presence, if need be, and in this
garden to-day. But as I have word of the time
and place about once a week I look not for it
now. However, I wear a shirt of mail under my
doublet, and my friends are here in good numbers, as also are those of my Lord of Arran. You
see, then, how the matter stands, but it would

not stay there long but for that woman in England. She has put me into this; and when the
time is ripe, and my life is in danger day and
night, she will not go on, but keeps our men on
the other side of the Border."

" And is the Captain Eviot one of the Master
of Gray's friends?" said a voice in interruption
of us, and the Earl of Arran stood by, gazing at
us with his head in the air, and an expression of
scorn on his face which would have provoked me
to laughter but that I knew the scorn to be
deep.

" I should have thought," said the other, drawing himself up in like manner with great dis-
daining—and I noticed that his right hand rested
on his dagger—"that any man in Scotland, even
my Lord of Arran, might speak to Captain Eviot
without offence."

" Well," replied the Earl, falling into proud
terms, " let him incur no scath."

" If he does," was the retort, " it will be from
your lordship, and not from the Master of
Gray."

Before any reply could be made to this plain
speech the King came out of the house, and a
cry of " To horse! to horse!" was raised. So
that in no great time the whole cavalcade set
forth for Falkland, but by way of Glendevon,

while special orders were given to M'Kuskan
Grossok and myself to attend the King as far as
the kirk-yard in the glen. A number of the
local gentry, also, for reasons of their own, set
out with us, being minded, in particular, to see
what order the King would take with Grossok.
And a gallant sight we made as we straggled up
Gleneagles, in which there is a stiff incline, with
steep hills on either side, and the bed of a torrent,
almost dry in summer, between them.

When we were half-way up the glen I was
directed to ride forward and speak with his
Majesty.

"It is even as you told us," said he; "we have
failed to make anything with the lassie Uchiltrie,
and we have taken some displeasure thereat, but
all to no purpose. It is not the first time we
have had ado with her on matters of importance,
though my Lord of Arran and his lady know it
not, and heretofore we have found her a maist
loyal and understanding subject. I am marvellous sorry she should question the right of her
Prince to her most inmost thoughts. But she
told me, man, a strange tale about a horse and a
ballad. Is that so?"

"The tale is true, sir, and this is the horse
which I am now riding."

"And a bonny beast it is—fit for a prince."

"It is at your disposal, sir, if you would deign to—"

"Na, na; we meant not that. We were thinking whether we have not with us one who was a friend of the poor man, and would ken his horse; and straunge it is I cannot come at one. And yet methinks the Laird of Duncrub, who is with us, might know."

The Laird of Duncrub was therefore summoned, and to him the King said:

"Duncrub, ye'll mind Geordie Uchiltrie, who was drowned in a bog, or fell down a coll-pit, or went some other gate of that sort?"

"I mind him well, sir; but I think not that he was drowned in a bog."

"What think ye came to him, then?"

"I think he was kidnapped."

"And who would kidnap him, man?" said the King, sharply.

"I cannot say, sir, because I do not know; but none the less I think he was kidnapped."

"Weel, if ye kenned the man, ye would ken his horse, for they tell me it was gey kenspeckle."

"I mind the horse well. The gentleman on the other side of your Highness is riding it at this moment."

"God's death!" exclaimed the King; "this is passing straunge."

"I had a mind, sir, to speak to the gentleman about it; but I was loath to dip in a matter which was no concern of mine. There are others in this country who have spoken of it to me. Peter Pardovine, of the Knowe, was for making a stir, and the miller at Dunning, and John Bonar, in the Kirkton of Mailer, came to me with the same story. But I told them to try and believe that they had never seen the horse, or they would come by the worse. For a time Captain Eviot suffered some prejudice in the minds of the country-folk on account of this horse; but since he broke out of the Tolbooth of Perth and fought Berald Stewart at Ruthven they will believe no evil of him."

"There is no evil in him, and ye may tell them that I said so. But, Duncrub, both you and he must be secret in this matter. We will smell out the truth of it ourselves; and it is better so, for the King has many sources of knowledge which other men know nothing of. And, indeed, we think that Heaven has specially endowed us with gifts which enable us to unravel such mysteries. But at one thing we are sorely grieved. There is no house more honorable in this land than the auld house of Duncrub; there is none who has been a more loyal subject and faithful friend to us than the Laird of Duncrub;

and yet our affairs are so mishandled that he is afraid to ask for justice. Our Council is rotten enough to ruin the whole realm."

"I would to God your Highness would alter it," was the blunt reply, "and that is the wish of most of your subjects."

"It's easy wishing," grumbled the King; "but, body o' me, man, who is to come in their place?"

CHAPTER XV

BEING now at the head of Gleneagles, where the water parts, to go one-half to the river Tay, and the other half to the Forth, we turned into Glendevon, than which I know no place in our country more gentle of aspect. Nowhere have the green hills, with their patches of heather, more grace of form. Down the glen runs a clear stream over a pebbly bed, through clumps of natural poplar, oak, and mountain-ash — to the eye a place little likely for the devices of the foul Fiend. Moreover, it lies apart from the highways of men, and withal so unpeopled that when all the homes in the small glens branching off it are told they would scarce furnish a congregation of twoscore for the minister's preaching. What place is this for the assembling of hell-dogs?

At the kirk, which is some distance down the glen, a halt was called, and the party, having dismounted, repaired to the kirk-yard. It was observed that his Highness on entering sniffed the air, coughed portentously, and frowned; but

12

having called for his afternoon and drunk it, he
sent for the irons of the kirk door, and without
more ado led the way inside. As many as could
find space followed him; but their admission was
no simple matter, for the capacity of the building was small, and the noblemen and gentlemen
in the King's company stood stiffly upon their
precedence.

There was much admiration when his Highness was seen to enter and take his seat in the
pulpit—a thing unlooked for, and not performed
without some protest on the part of the minister.
Mr. James Pyott, having been duly warned by
the King of his intended visit, was present, and
remonstrated as far as he might; and although
I was too far distant to hear what was said, I
could see that some warm passages were exchanged between him and the King. I believe
that the latter, while admitting his duty to
sit among the congregation during preaching,
prayer, or praise, contended that he had a right,
as head of the Kirk, to occupy the pulpit when
investigating a matter proper to his function.
Not much stir was made about this intrusion at
the time, because the firebrands of the Kirk were
for the most part among the Peregrine Ministers
in England. But Mr. Craig, the King's minister,
preaching the following Sabbath, sharply admon-

ished his Highness in respect of the same, declaring that it smelled of Popery, and was prompted by his godless and villanous Council. At the moment, however, little heed was given to what Mr. Craig said, although my Lord of Arran did threaten him with his dagger when he spoke these words.

"How comes it, Mr. James," cried the King from his seat, "that ye have not cleared the auld rotten Papistry out of this house of God? Yonder is a stone font—we like not the look of it; and here are some straunge letters carved on the back of an oaken chair. And if our eyes deceive us not, we can perceive the figure of some sanct rudely done in relief and let into the eastern end of the kirk. Maybe it will be meant for the blessed Servanus; the poor bodie hath a brig named after him in this glen. It was even he, if we mistake not, who cured a chiel who had miskenned his appetite by putting a dirty thumb down his throat. Moreover, we can see mony odds and ends of other Popish baggage brushed away into the corner yonder.

"It is mair nor twenty years," he continued, "since their filthy religion was swept out of Scotland, but its roots are not dead in this glen, as it seems."

"I knew not, sir," said the minister, being

somewhat confused, "that these were emblems of sin. And I think not that my flock has suffered from their presence here, for no one has regarded them."

"Daur ye to tell me, sir, that your flock has not suffered?" cried the King, growing red with indignation. "Sma' wonder that this is weel kenned to be the maist witch-ridden place in Scotland, when the minister hoards these memorials of the Man of Sin in the kirk, and the haill kirk-yard smells maist damnably of fire and brimstone. Ye will not tell me, sir, that ye have not heard the accounts we speak of?"

"I have indeed heard them, but I looked upon them as idle tales, fabricated by auld wives."

"By auld witches, mair like. Having the cure of maybe less than forty souls, have ye ever visited your kirk at the appointed time to see if there be ony truth in these tales?"

"The appointed time?"

"Aye, the witching hour."

"No, sir, the hour is midnight, when all honest men ought to be abed."

"And very good law for slowbellies and country parsons. But we take no delight in being large; so we would have ye hear one who can maybe tell ye mair about your kirk-yard than ye ken yourself. Where awa' is the chiel Grossok? Ah! man, are ye there? Is it Grossok they ca' ye?"

" Maister M'Kuskan Grossok, if it please your Majesty."

" Maister, indeed! And which of our Universities made ye Maister? But I needna ask, for I would wager my crown to a gray groat that it was St. Andrews. Ye will be saying next that ye are a minister."

" Aye, a minister of the Gospel. Your Majesty is right. I was laureated at St. Andrews."

" What!" screamed the King, " a minister of the Gospel! Of whose gospel, sir?"

" Of the Gospel of Christ."

" Mair like to be the gospel of hell," muttered the King, regaining his composure. " Ye'll ken, Maister Grossok, if ye were educated at St. Andrews, that the deil has a gospel or book of his ain. Have ye ever had a sight of it?"

" I know it not, sir."

" It is a book, they tell me—them that has seen it—which has braw pictures of men and women and castles, the sun, moon, and stars, and suchlike."

" I may have seen the cards, sir, but not to handle or to have any skill in them."

" So it seems. But have ye skill to cast a horoscope, or any gift of divination, by which ye might foretell future events, or maybe speir where stolen gear is, as it might be jewels or precious stones?"

The man looked ill at ease, for the King began to press him so close that he could scarce doubt that some one had betrayed him. He glanced at my Lord of Arran, whose countenance, however, showed nothing but extreme indifference.

"I would I had such a gift; it might be useful to your Majesty and other honest folk," he replied, at last.

"Weel," said the King, "for all the good it has done us it seems ye have it not, though that gives us no assurance that ye have not tried it. But ye have heard that this place is given up at unlawful hours to witches and warlocks. Ye'll no deny that ye ken the place. Ye have been here before?"

"Aye, I ken the place weel enough."

"Ye have been here at night, man. What hour was it?"

"It was midnight."

"Aye," said the King, eagerly, apparently much interested, "and what did ye see?"

"I saw nothing, sir, if it were not a howlet or twa in the dark trees."

"But ye ken the character of the place at

yon hour? Was there nobody here but yourself?"

"Nobody but myself and the howlets."

"And what manner of man did ye come to
see? Ye expected to see somebody?"

"I didna ken who might be here. I came to
see if a' tales were true."

"Weel, if ye ken the place, ye'll have seen the
big trout in the pool yonder?"

"Aye, I saw him ance. He was lying under
a stane, with his heid out at one end and his
tail at the other; but he lookit no different from
ony other big trout."

"And what thought ye—that he was going
up and down the water about his ain business,
or that he was possessed by some evil power?"

"I thought he wasna canny."

"What made ye think that?"

"Weel, there's no a man about the country-side
who hasna tried to catch the creature, and I
have heard that the minister, who angled with
the best of them, ance hookit it as he supposed.
But it first dragged him into the water and
almost drowned him. Then the muckle beast
loupit out as it would have bitten him, and running down the top of the water never stopped
until it came to the mill at Downhill."

"Some ministers," said the King, gravely,

" would catch men, and some would catch rats. For this pastime, we have not as yet demeanit ourselves to it; but from what other folks have told us we see nothing in this to signify possession by any infernal power."

" Maybe no," retorted Grossok; " but when the minister recovered his tackle it was tied in sic knots as only the deil himsel' could have fashioned. And Mr. Pyott didna doubt that he had had ado with something mair than earthly."

Mr. James Pyott grew very red in the face while this tale was being told; but, being called upon, he could not deny that it was true.

His Highness thereupon made some speech at large upon the filthy and abominable practice of witchcraft, which was most damnable in a man, seeing that rather women, and especially old women, being of a weaker nature, were prone to it. He shrewdly suspected that Maister Grossok (whom he styled a trout-spying, kirk-yard thief) knew further in the matter; and desired that, until he should be better informed, the diviner should find strong caution for his behavior. Whereupon the Earl of Arran, who seemed to be disturbed by the course of the conversation, agreed to be cautioner, and the party dissolved once more into the kirk-yard.

There were some godless men at the King's

Court at this time who believed neither in God nor devil, and these, when their master's back was turned, spoke of this scene with ridicule and blasphemous laughter. But the greater portion of those present believed firmly in the power of the fiend, and liked not the matter at all.

I have often been asked in later years what I thought of my master's course on this occasion. For myself, I believe that he has no more doubt than I have of the power of the enemy of man to work for evil through perverted men and women. And I verily believe that he looked upon this place as bewitched, as it is in fact at this day. But even at his early age he was a very deep man, whose mind no one could fathom. He took a strange delight in scenes, some of them ludicrous, which mystified those who were about him. And I think that he had a twofold purpose in this visit to Glendevon. He deeply enjoyed the solemn perplexity on the faces of the men about his Court, many of whom he knew to be profligate blasphemers. But his main purpose was in a circuitous manner to bring home to my Lady Arran and Grossok that it would not be safe for them to go further in their dealings with the Evil One. For he fully believed that the powers of evil might be invoked by human agency to work ruin to mankind and to himself among others.

Those of us who parted here from his Highness rode down Gleneagles that night a goodly
company; for which I was glad, because I had
not forgotten the card which the abominable
Grossok turned up the night I looked in at the
window, nor the rhyme which he professed to
repeat about the kirk-yard of Glendevon. And
when we rode out of the glen into the lowland
of Strathearn I drew a long breath of relief.

When we had ferried the Earn, and had now
no great distance to go, a little crimson light
grew up into the sky to the east; and, as
it began to spread, I turned to Carryg, and
said:

"Surely, David, it is early in the season to be
burning the undergrowth."

"Yon's no undergrowth, sir."

"What is it, then, if it be not St. Johnston,
with its amiable Tolbooth, that burns?"

"It will be buildings of some sort, but no St.
Johnston, which is farther fra us by twa miles
than yon fire."

"Nothing cheats the eye, David, more than
the reflection of fire in the sky. Multiply the
distance as it seems to your eye by four, and
you will not be far wrong."

"I am reckoning that, sir."

"Then, great God! man, do you mean that

that is the castle? Ride up, lads; for the love of God, ride!"

Long before we rode into Ruthven the truth was only too plain. The castle was on fire. On reaching the spot we found much people collected, who, for the most part, looked on with marvelling eyes. The western wing was in flames throughout the whole of its lower part; but the wind setting from the southeast, the eastern tower, in which I was lodged, was untouched, and likely to remain so. The efforts of man, therefore, could avail but little; so the crowd stood by while the castle burned. The upper part of the burning building was not yet affected, but the flames were working steadily upward, and all access was cut off from below.

I marvelled somewhat when I perceived my Lady and her party fully equipped for departure, her horses and baggage being in appearance complete. She, at least, had taken no scath by the fire. Making bold to address her, I asked whether all had escaped from the castle, to which she replied "Yea." And on my saying that I saw not Mistress Jean or her woman, she said that they were safe, but in a manner so strange and cold that I felt ill at ease.

Whereupon I inquired of others who stood by, and finding that none had seen or had any knowledge of Mistress Jean's escape, I ran forthwith to the keep in which I was lodged. And having entered with some doubt that all was not well, by the time I reached the parapet I was sick at heart with fear.

Truly it marvelled me to see the plank thrown across between the two parapets, but it gave me some relief; for here, at the worst, was a bridge of escape, though a mere lass was scarce like to have the head to cross it.

In less than a second I was on the parapet of the burning castle; and remembering the mistake I had made the last time I was there, turned to the left, and ran quickly round to the southern side. Here, finding an open window, I stepped into an apartment, from which, as I was entering, I saw the figure of a woman pass quickly out by the door. She was scarce gone when I ran through the same door, only to see her escape through the window of the adjacent apartment. Quick as thought I sped out of the window—I was so close upon her I might almost have caught her dress—but once out I could see her nowhere. She could not have gone by the parapet, for I must have seen her before she turned the corner, whether she took to the right or the left. There was no door or window by which she could have regained the building. She could not have clambered on to the roof. There was only one thing left, and that was not credible. Jean—for I felt assured it was she—could not have thrown herself from the parapet.

Then I clean lost my head. I searched every corner and recess in the roof, calling "Jean! Jean!" at the full of my voice; but naught came back from the rafters but the echo of my own cry. Could God let such things be—that one in the flesh should vanish on the moment into thin air? In a frenzy of wonder, fear, and grief I ran from one part to another, crying aloud for Jean; but the only answer I got was a dull, lifeless, mechanical "Jean" from the walls.

The flames were now beginning to lick up to the plank, my only hope of escape, and the place became very hot. I could do no more, but with what reluctance I came away I can scarce tell. I soon found that no one had fallen from the parapet and been dashed to death on the ground below. But I know not that this discovery gave me rest; for it left me to think that the same power which had taken the apostle Peter through four quaternions of soldiers had passed Jean Uchiltrie from the top of Ruthven Castle, or that she was being burned alive at that moment in some secret part of the building.

My Lady and her people had slipped away,

nobody knew in what direction, or by whom accompanied, and I was left for the moment in possession of what remained of Ruthven Castle. But so clouded was my mind by what had happened that I felt I could think of nothing until I had certainty upon one point. I must know whither my Lady had gone and who had gone with her. I must have the truth about Jean Uchiltrie before I did anything else in this world. So, tired as our horses were, I had them saddled again, and rode forth upon the King's road towards Stirling.

CHAPTER XVI

As I thought, my Lady's party had taken the road to Stirling. I had knowledge of this not many minutes after leaving the castle, and again at Auchterarder. It was strange, however, that one spoke of a company of six persons, while another put the number as high as twenty, and the report at Auchterarder was that there were but two women of the party. As we rode on we got no further information, for the night was far spent and nobody was stirring.

So we came at last, as the day began to break, to a point at no great distance from the North Brig of Stirling, and it behooved us to go no farther in that direction. By the tracks on the road, seen in the first rays of the rising sun, we could tell that the party had turned neither to the right nor the left, but gone straight for the Brig; but we might not follow them, for two reasons. The Brig was closed for ordinary passengers, and my Lord of Arran was Captain of the Castle. Andrew Eviot would have had short shrift in Stirling on that day. So we turned

aside into the Earl of Mar's country, and sought
the house of a yeoman of whom I had certain
intelligence.

My Lord of Mar was one of the Banished
Lords, and at that moment was living perforce
in London. But for these Banished Lords the
rule of Bloody Haman and his wicked Jezabel
would have been absolute in Scotland; and for
that reason urgent appeals had been made to
the English Court for their surrender. But the
Queen of England, learning from the anxiety of
my Lord of Arran that she held an important
card in her hand, followed her usual custom.
She kept the card in her hand, and not all the
entreaties of her best advisers could induce her
to use it either for or against the exiles. So my
Lord of Arran continued to be *Dominus Fac-
totum* in the Court of the King my master; but
he lived in the daily dread of the return of the
men who could pluck him from his place. And
so time drifted.

But during this time there was constant and
daily communication held between these Lords
and their friends in Scotland. In sooth, the posts
between the two countries have never ridden so
regularly either before or since, and yet on both
sides they were prohibited. My Lord Hunsdon
complained bitterly of the strange riding from

Newcastle into Scotland, and out of Scotland
again, but he could not stop it. Now there were
certain houses, known only to those who had
secret intelligence, where the friends of the exiled men were welcomed, and of these was the
house where I now sought shelter.

It was noon before I awoke the following
morning. As I had no mind to sleep out my
time there, I was soon stirring, and began by
explaining to my host what I required. It was
not possible for me or either of my men to enter
openly into Stirling; but we found that, clothed
in some of my host's old garments, I made a
reasonably good yeoman, while John Sloan was
with no great difficulty so apparelled that none
would have taken him for anything but a hind.
So John Sloan and I went on our way towards
Stirling, the one disguised as a yeoman, the other
as a hind. We crossed to the south side of the
Forth in a crazy boat, nigh to the place of Alloa,
and in time came on foot to the West Port of
Stirling, by which we entered the town.

And we had no difficulty in assuring ourselves
of the information we sought, for all knew that
my Lady had entered the night before and passed
into the castle, and that there were but two
women in the party. This news discouraged
me, but I feared some trick had been played
13

upon me, and was not yet satisfied that I was on a wrong scent.

We chanced, as we were on the point of leaving the town, to see a thing which is of but too common occurrence in the great towns of this country. One, stripped naked of clothing, was scourged from the West Port to the Brig End, and there thrust out of the Port, with a warning not to return to the town upon the pain of death.

I knew not what this poor wretch had done. I had bade John Sloan inquire; but the first he spoke to shook his head and moved away without answer, and the second said, " If ye are on fameeliar tearmes wi' my Lord Arran, wha keeps the castle yonder, ye might speir at him. Naebody else in this toun kens. But if I was ye, man, I wouldna speir at onybody." Well, I think there are some crimes for which I could flog a man with my proper hand, for they make my blood boil. In some things reasoning is a waste of breath, and I would not argue with any man whether my instinct is right here; though well I know that there are men whose blood never boils.

But knowing not the nature of this poor man's offence, the terrible suffering inflicted on him caused a great pity to arise in me. The lash cut through the skin, and coming back upon the same spots widened the wounds until there was not an inch of sound skin remaining on his back. We are apt to pass by with closed eyes the extremes of human þain ; but I was moved to follow this man to the end of his castigation, because through it all he flinched not once. Nor did he give one sob, or sigh, or dolorous sign. I have seen men do acts of great bravery and courage, but I have known nothing more approaching to heroism than the demeanor of this man.

When the scourgers had done their office, and were about to thrust him out of the Port, one of the poorer sort, a woman, cast a cloth over him to cover his nakedness. Perchance she had a son, or a husband, or a brother, who had suffered the like treatment. She had followed with the rest of us to the Port, and when she had cast the cloth upon him she went her ways, looking not for thanks, nor regarding those who stood by. Surely the great God seeth these things, and some treasure is laid up for those who do them, where neither moth nor rust do corrupt, nor thieves break through and steal. It hath often moved me to see how quick the poor are to show compassion. Every stroke of the lash I had felt on my own back, and yet had I not as much thought for the object of my pity as this poor woman.

With some feeling of indignation that one who had shown himself a man indeed should be thus mishandled, we left the town as we entered it; but for some cause which I remember not now we returned to our quarters by a different route. After going a few miles up the river we crossed to the north side, and so came down the water-side to the spot whence we started in the morning. But when we had passed the Stirling Brig by no great distance I noticed an object of unusual appearance at no great distance from the track; and being curious to know what it might be, I found on approaching that it was no other than the poor creature whom we had seen scourged through the streets of Stirling. He was crouching in an attitude of the deepest dejection, his elbows resting on his knees and his face buried in his hands.

"Cheer up, man," said I, "and give not the devil a chance now. One who can take his fortune as we saw you an hour or two ago must be of better spirit than to sit upon the ground like this."

Thereupon he lifted up his face (which I had not yet seen, for I walked behind him when he was scourged), and I marvelled indeed to see that this man was Barabbas, the servitor of the Earl of Arran, and my constant companion for some time past.

"I see, sir," said he, "that ye knew me not. Nor know ye my occasion. For the bodily pain and the shame done to me, I have endurit them, and they count for little — though truly I am sa sair woundit that I could scarce walk from this spot if I would. But I have lost my employment, and nane will readily take a man to serve him who has been with the Earl of Arran. I care not for myself; but I have a mother, a widowed woman, living in Halidayhill, who hath depended these ten years past wholly upon me. And what I may do for her now, poor woman, God alone knoweth." And this man, who had not so much as winked an eye under the most terrible punishment, burst into a flood of tears.

"Give not way to this," I replied; "be a man still; and albeit I have not been without some grudge against you" (here he looked curiously at me), "because I know you to be a man I will not desert you. I will have you taken from hence to a place where you may remain until you recover from your wounds, and will give you wherewithal to maintain and clothe you until you are able to seek a new master for yourself."

The sight of this uncouth creature in tears, while not without something of the ludicrous, was strangely pitiable. And indeed, as I said,

I had him taken from where he was to a certain cottage, where he was to lie until he was recovered. And, being a temperate man, and living much in God's fresh air, he made a quick recovery.

Meanwhile I continued for a few days in the same spot, making such inquiries as I might in different parts, including the vicinity of Kinneil. For I still thought that a trick had been played upon me, in the hope that I might seek elsewhere when I knew that but two women had passed from Ruthven Castle to Stirling on the night of the fire. But I could gain no intelligence; and being satisfied at length that I was on the wrong track, I ordered my horse to be saddled, meaning to return to Ruthven, which indeed I should never have left.

While, then, my horse was being saddled, and preparations were made for our departure, to my great surprise Barabbas stood before me. Though he could scarce have put his garment on his back without enduring great agony, he had arisen and come forth to speak with me.

"I heard, sir," said he, "that ye had ordered your horse to be saddled. I felt I couldna be left behind if I might get your permission to go with ye."

This would never do. I had had enough of

supervision from Barabbas, and wished for no more. Besides, though I now knew him to be a brave man, it did not follow that he was a true man.

"Nay," I replied, "that may not be. For, to begin, your back must still be so sore that you could not possibly travel. Then I am a man of no great substance, and though for the present I can make such show as I do, I cannot be at the charge of another man."

"As to that, sir, I would serve for a season without wages. I have received unlooked-for kindness from ye, and would show that I am grateful."

"In the third place, Barabbas, I have my own particular affairs to attend to, and for the present, at least, they cannot be set forward by those who are strangers to them."

"Ah!" he replied, with some reproach in his voice, "'twas but likely that ye should distrust me, for I served one who endeavored to do ye much evil. But that service is over, indeed, as ye can well credit, having seen what ye did."

"Aye, it is like, indeed; but it marvels me that I asked you not before for what cause did my Lord use you in this despiteful fashion?"

"Joshua Henderson put him first in suspicion of me about a letter which the loon said I ripped

from yon body by the Clochrigstane. Ye'll mind
the rider that came clattering down the brae
when I fetched him out of his saddle?"

" I remember it well. I saw you take the
letter."

" Ye saw me? Well, I didna think there was
a man alive could have seen that."

" I have sharp eyes, and I wonder not that my
Lord took you in suspicion if he knew it."

" He knew it not for truth. But ye, at least,
Captain Eviot, can scarce complain, for found ye
not the letter in your gauntlet at Falkland?
And long before we came to the Clochrigstane
had not the letters to his Highness and the Laird
of Kilsyth been exchanged, the one for the other?"

" How know you that, man?" said I, sharply.

" Because I shifted them mysel'."

At which reply I was somewhat startled. I
had thought this Barabbas a cunning, spying
man, but I had not looked for such adroitness as
this from him. If he were so deep in these matters, perchance he knew more of my designs and
doings than I thought for. But I could scarce
run the risk of sounding him further than he
chose to go of his own accord.

" I have been of service to ye," he continued,
" mair often than ye ken; maybe I might serve
ye again if I but get the chance. We who serve

ken mair than is thought, both of our master's business and the business of other folk. Because we do not speak our silence is oft taken for ignorance. But if ye would not take it for presumption I would make bold to say that Captain Eviot requires my service."

" Tut, tut, man ; what do you know ?"

" If I were to say, sir, what I know it might hurt others, therefore I will hold my peace. But if ye will take me I will do ye no scath, and may do ye service as good as I have done before."

" Nay, friend Barabbas," said I, irritated by his persistence, " I will have no one about me or in my service who tells me that he will keep his knowledge to himself. I want no one whom I cannot trust or who cannot trust me. So fish for yourself, and in your own waters."

But the creature continued to plead with so much persistency and humility, vowing fidelity, and asserting his power to serve me, that at last, because of his importunity, I consented to allow him to ride with me back to Ruthven Castle, but no farther. So we procured for him a sorry-looking hackney, which seemed to be but skin and bone, and mounted him thereon. And the hackney, for all that it had such an ill appearance, held its own with the other horses, and when it made Ruthven Castle was as fresh as when it started.

CHAPTER XVII

IF my Lady Jezabel had failed to recover the X Jewel it seemed that she had at least thrown me out of the chase. I had lost her presence for the moment if not for always, and thus I could no longer run with the hound that would always be near the hare. I might follow my Lady at a distance, but she would never again endeavor to use me as a tool.

It was possible she knew as little of Mistress Jean's fate as I did, but in my heart I knew that that could scarce be true. I had not thrown off the feeling that I had been tricked, but where and how I could not find. As to the jewel—time alone would show whether I was in the right or not; but I still believed that to find Jean Uchiltrie was to recover the mistress of the jewel, and I had come back to the spot where I lost her, resolute to follow her step by step until I knew the truth. But no intelligence did I get from the indwellers on the spot which was of any use to me. Nobody had been found in the buildings after the fire abated, and none believed that life had been lost; but, unhappily, that proved nothing. On the following morning I sent my men into the neighboring villages, but they brought back nothing beyond the vague, distracted rumors which the rustic brain delights to fabricate.

Meantime I set myself to examine with great care the fabric of the burned-out building. And I took upon hand to do this because none was present who had power or occasion to hinder me. The Chancellor's folk had abandoned the place, and my Lord of Montrose had not entered upon the possession of it; so, albeit the commission I carried in my pouch was but for a shift, I made it serve my turn on this occasion.

The fire had cleared out all that was combustible in the upper part of the castle; but inasmuch as the walls were of great thickness and strength, and the turnpike-stairs built of stone, but little harm was done to the permanent frame of the building. There was nothing to hinder me from ascending by the winding staircase to the parapet, and thither I did indeed go, Carryg and Sloan being absent from the castle on my business, and Barabbas having disappeared, bent on some particular of his own. When I had been engaged for some space in examining every visible inch of the structure, with a view to detect some

secret arrangement in it, but so far without success, I found myself on a sudden face to face
with Barabbas. I was not surprised that he
should follow me there, for I thought him of a
prying disposition; but for a moment it gave
me a scare to think that he had not come up by
the turnpike-stair, which was the only means of
ascending to the parapet. M'Kuskan Grossok
might come up on a broomstick for aught that I
knew, or in the form of a carrion-crow, but I
had scarce reckoned Barabbas among the devil's
bairns. The staircase was behind me, and I had
assured myself that there was no one else on the
parapet; and yet as I was busied with my work
—there was Barabbas in front of me.

I had had time to ponder upon this man's tale
and to question to what purpose he had inter-
fered in my business. I had resolved that he
should purge himself on that point, if he would
speak on no other. But when I found him
again upon my track, not being bidden thereto,
I thought I should let him see who was master.

"What do you here," I cried, harshly, "without leave and without orders from me? And by
what road came you hither? Answer me that."

"I came by the gate I have aye used, Captain."

I was not willing he should guess what was in
my mind on that head, so I again demanded

to know for what purpose he had sought me there.

"E'en to deliver this letter into your hands," he replied, giving me a letter directed in a hand which I knew right well, and bearing these words on the back: "Ride, ride, for your life, for your life, for your life!" A rude gallows was traced in the corner, and the following indorsement had been freshly written on it: "Received at the Castell of Ruthven, an hour before Noon, this 19th day of July 1585."

"Who made this indorsement?" said I.

"I did, sir."

"And how dare you do that? How dare you take upon yourself to handle a letter directed to me? You are not in my service, and methinks, friend Barabbas, your fingers are over nimble with other folks' writings. I begin to find how you came by that scourging at Stirling. And, hark ye: if ye have not more care ye will come by something worse than scourging."

"I did it for the best, sir. Your men were absent, none knew where ye were, and I would not folk should ken. The post was pressed for time, and if I had not taken the letter he might have left it with those whose eyes are mair curious than mine. As you ken weel, an ill-delivered letter seldom comes to the hands of its rightful owner in this country. Moreover, although ye trust me not, maybe the writer of this letter does." And he mentioned a name which I would fain not have heard from his lips.

"You are an over-presuming knave, and as you will not leave my business alone you will be good enough to explain how you came to interfere in it. What made you tamper with the letters of my Lord of Arran? What made you ram the Laird of Kilsyth's letter into my gauntlet at Falkland? It was not for love of me. What was it, man? If you had desisted, I might have let you pass; but as I find you still in my path, and you have no longer my Lord of Arran to please, you leave not this spot until you have given me an answer."

"I confess, sir, that I came hither for another purpose besides the delivery of yon letter. I had but to bide below, and I had not incurred your anger; but I canna forget your kindness to me. I was poor and hungry, and ye clothed and fed me; I was sick, and ye tended me; I was bruised and broken in spirit, and ye gave me courage. And these are things a Border lad never forgets. So I made bold to face your anger; and now I would anger ye still further, though if ye could but think me a true man to you there would be no just cause for anger."

"What's all this talk about? Speak up, man."

" I would not be thought to pry into your reasons. In the performance of my service accident made me acquaint with some of your particular affairs; but that was not my fault, and I have used my knowledge only to your advantage. I seek not to know your purpose in coming hither; but this I would say, in the hope it may save ye some trouble and anxiety: if ye seek here any person or any thing, ye waste your time; for both she and it are elsewhere, and in sure keeping."

His meaning was plain enough to me, though his words were veiled. Was it possible for me to pretend to misunderstand him?

" Speak plainly, man," I said. " Of whom and what do you speak? There is none to overhear you here."

" I'm no so sure o' that," he replied, looking suspiciously round, and seeming to peer between the joints of the masonry. " As for the lady, I needna name her; ye will surely ken my meaning without that. But as for the gear, there is no reason why it should not be named between us, for it is well known to both of us—in plain Scots, the X Jewel."

" Ah!" said I, jeeringly, for I believed him not, saying to myself that he would gain what he could of my knowledge, "so this lady and this jewel are in sure keeping. Where, may I ask?"

"As for the lady, I can say no more but that she is in safety."

"Of course you cannot. You are a lying knave, and I suppose your knowledge of the jewel goes not beyond your formula that it is in safe keeping."

"I have it myself, and that is sure enough."

"What, you rascal!" I cried, losing all sense of caution in the surprise and anger of the moment, "do you boast of having in your keeping one of the royal jewels stolen from the King's jewel-chest?"

"It's no a royal jewel," he replied, contemptu-ously; "it's but a piece of filthy Papistry; but it's in good keeping, sure enough, and there it will bide for a while."

"Not so, cozening knave. If you don't hand it over to me on the spot, I will call up Carryg and Sloan, and we will hang you from the para-pet without more ado. So you can begin your prayers as soon as you like."

"That wouldna do ye much good, sir; for ye will likely ken that I would not be speaking so blithely of yon gear if I had it about me. It's in sure keeping now; but if I am hangit, maybe the secret of its hiding-place would die with me."

"This passes all endurance," I cried; "if I cannot bring you to reason, I will take you to his Majesty."

I know not what I should have made of him if I had taken him then and there. I might have thrown him into the dungeon below the castle until he gathered his manners, or I might have ridden over with him to Falkland and delivered him out of hand to the King. But as I stepped forward, making as I would have seized him, he slipped behind the masonry of the window and seemed to disappear into the stone.

This is passing strange, thought I, as I went forward to examine the place, but the mystery was soon explained. Behind a stone which was somewhat larger than its neighbors was a clumsily shaped gap in the masonry of space sufficient to admit the body of a person of middle size. On coming close to the aperture and looking into it I could see that a rude staircase of narrow compass descended somewhat precipitously, and I doubted not that it led to the base of the building. Perhaps I should have come upon it if my search had not been interrupted; but there was small wonder that I did not discover it on the evening of the fire, for it was clev-

14

erly concealed, the light was bad, and I was greatly excited. It was here that the woman I saw vanished, and it was by means of this stair that Barabbas had intercepted me a few minutes before, when I was examining the parapet.

I was debating whether I should descend and endeavor to catch him below, for I had no mind to venture my person in this rat-hole, when I heard a little cry, as of an animal when it is caught in a gin. A sort of disturbed sound also came from the secret passage, such as is made by weasels and conies when they engage each other beneath the ground. As the sound seemed to approach me I waited a space, and erelong the form of Barabbas retreated backward forth of the passage, dragging with him some object as he came.

"Here's a precious vermin!" he cried, as I recognized the ferret features of M'Kuskan Grossok. "I kent there were open lugs about, but it's well it happened no waur. The place is convenient, and none will guess that he didna fall or throw himself down, like Judas Iscariot, for he hath been a sinful body." And without more ado he swung Grossok over the parapet, and held him suspended by the collar.

"Give him five seconds for his prayers," said I.

"Mercy! For the love of Christ, spare me!"

cried the wretched man. "I will tell everything, on my great oath."

"Pull him up for a moment and swear him. I will give him a chance for his life."

Barabbas, with some show of dissatisfaction, drew him over the parapet again, trembling and with the fear of death upon him, and swore him upon a copy of the Gospels which, to my astonishment, he produced from his pouch.

"Now," said I, "how came you here?"

"By yon passage."

"Aye, but who sent you, and what was your purpose? Tell me the truth, and I will spare your life. If you lie, over you go."

"Nobody sent me. My Lady would know where a certain chain was, and what had come of Mistress Jean Uchiltrie, of whom she had no tidings since the fire here. And, having some skill of divination, I—"

"You came here to pry out with your ferret's eyes and your rascally lugs what the devil wouldn't tell you. Now, mark me, sirrah, for on the truth of your answer to this question your life depends—what is this chain you speak of, and what hath my Lady to do with it?"

"It is a chain with a jewel hanging fra it which has been callit the X, and was at one time in my Lady's hands; but it has been reft fra her."

"So be it; you seem to have spoken the truth, and you have not taken much by your pains. None the less, this manner of divination deserveth some recompense, and ye shall not be cheated of it."

"Shall I put him over, sir?" said Barabbas, with alacrity. I think that Barabbas had many old scores to pay off upon this man, to whose chattering tongue he owed his disgrace and dismissal from the Earl of Arran's service. Moreover, he knew that Grossok had probably overheard his admission that he had the X Jewel; and he rightly feared that if the tale got abroad he would become an object of my Lady Arran's most solicitous care. But I saw no disadvantage in that, because I reckoned that it would force him to open his hand to me.

"No, no," replied I; "I meant not that."

"Dead folk winna bite; and this one, if he lives, will bite like a viper."

"I cannot have it, man. Bring him down in the meantime."

And, to be short, the wretched man was cast into the castle dungeon, where he remained for some hours. When Carryg and Sloan returned I was able to attend to him according to his merits; for, causing the three men to mount their horses, I bade them chase the creature from the place, keeping him on the trot for the space of three miles or so, and giving him an occasional taste of their horse-wands. I learned some time afterwards that the rascals had the insolence to exceed their authority; for not only did they flog the diviner most unmercifully, but they cropped his ears before they let him go.

This was a lucky adventure for Barabbas, for ere I could speak further with him I had gone somewhat from my anger, and I listened to him with some patience.

"Sir," said he, when he could approach me again, "ye may send me to the King if ye will, but that will not serve. I ken, of course, I should be booted; but ye have seen enough of me to know that the torture will not make me speak. If I could but make ye believe it, the King will draw nothing from me that I will not tell to you. And after I am booted, who would be the better? My Lord and Lady, and yonder Grossok ye have with too much mercy spared, would be weel content; but ye would lose a servant whose help, I ken weel, ye will want, and, moreover, it is an ill moment for you, sir, to repair to the Court."

"Why so?"

"Maybe the letter I brought ye some time since will give ye news." I had forgotten the letter for the moment, and yet from the extravagances on the back of it I was to suppose it was urgent. Dismissing Barabbas, I broke open the despatch, wherein I read as follows:

"RIGHT TRAIST FREIND,—It needs that I see you quickly, for the cause is in straits and wanteth you. All at this Court walk in greate daunger, insomuch than none goeth without his pistols, and I enter not even the King's presence except I am well attended by my friends. These things cannot endure, and it behooveth us to be the first to strike. I now see clearly that we shall lose our Latin except we contrive a lasting breach between the Queen of England and Bloody Haman; and, as I shall show you when we meet, you are the instrument chosen for the work. But our occasion is of days, nay, of hours, for the King inclineth to this league with England; and if he sign it with the great Bloodsucker by his side we must make a run of it. For though his Highness greatly affecteth me, he will not allow a hair of the other's head to be injured.

"For our tryst 'twere best you came not here; for, seeing the work we have in hand, I would have none know that I speak with you, and none know that you come into Fyff, or that you go thence. For if that be known your passing to the South might chance to be more lively than you look for. Come, therefore, under the darkness of night, and meet me an hour before sunrise to-morrow morning on St. Serf's Inch, in Lochleven. Bring all and everything with you; for if I know you rightly you will scarce return to your enchanted castell now that the birds have flown. A boat will await you at the southeastern extremity of the Loch which you may trust to carry you to the Inch, but let not those who guide it set their foot on the island. At Falkland, this 19th day of July 1585.—Your veric affectionat freind to do you service."

This letter was without signature, but it needed no signature for me.

CHAPTER XVIII

THE air grows cold upon St. Serf's Inch an hour before sunrise. I, who have been there at such an hour, albeit on a summer morning, should know. For half an hour I had crouched among the reeds on the northern edge of the island, straining my eyes towards the shore. But to no purpose, for a murky gloom hung over the loch, and there was no thin streak of light in the east such as usually precedes the dawn. The water was as smooth as polished glass, and there was not a breath of wind. There was a dead silence, and it grew colder.

Then there was a faint stirring of the reeds; I could hear them jostle each other; and a light breeze grew over the water and rippled it. A tinge of crimson crept on to the horizon to the east, but it would be some time yet ere the sun rose. Here and there came a single chirrup from a small bird, or a croak from a cock grouse which had been roused too soon, and ducks began to fly across the Inch in twos and threes.

It was still very dark, for the murk was thick upon the water.

Then there came from the loch, but, as it seemed, close to the island and very low, the note of the thrush. I suppose the thrush visits the Inch, but it does not pipe on the water in the cold hours of the morning. So I returned the note, and when a few seconds had passed I saw the nose of a boat glide out of the gloom and make the shore but a few paces from me. A tall, slim man sprang from the bow, and desired those who had brought him to remain by their oars, and on no account to land or leave the boat. When he turned I was standing at his elbow, and, dark as it was, we had no need of light to see each other; but he was careful not to name me, nor did I name him.

This Inch, once, as it is said, the site of a monastery founded by the Culdees, is now wholly given up to pasturage for cattle; but inasmuch as it extends to ninety acres or so of ground, and is not encumbered with trees or brushwood, it is not unsuited for secret converse.

"Andrew," said this stranger, when he had drawn me by the arm out of all danger of being overheard, "I am late. I had great difficulty in winning clear of them. This is a strange place for a tryst, is it not?"

"Aye," I said; "surely you might have saved us the trouble of the boats and the danger of babbling from the owners of them?"

"Nay, I think I have done well. Our purpose is ruined if they know that I have met you; for even if your adventure succeeds it would be worse than useless to us if they know it to be done by you. Now I think not that you have been tracked hither; but I have been closely haunted for some days past, so that I was sore put to it to get free. It happened, however, some years ago, when I was at Rome and unregenerate, that one calling himself the Bishop of Ross gave me the secret of certain passages which lead from the Prior's House at St. Andrews to the Haven. The knowledge thereof is now to few; but as I could not, without spiting our purpose, come away openly, I made my exit underground. Doubtless they still watch the place, and will be there to-morrow morning when I am disjuning at Falkland."

"But we might have met in the fields."

"We might; but if I have been tracked hither there is a better chance of your escaping unknown than if we were observed together in the fields. And that is the important point. Now, listen, for we may not stay many minutes; we must not be seen here."

He had need to be quick, for the crimson glow in the east was growing larger and deeper in tint, and the clamor from the birds on the shores of the loch had become almost deafening. But it was still very dark.

"Here, Andrew," continued my friend, "is a safe-conduct for you when you are across the Border, which will be to-night, if I mistake not, or to-morrow morning. And this is a letter you will deliver to the Master of Glamis."

"To London!" said I, in some dismay.

"Nay, to Newcastle. I forgot you would scarce know, for it hath been kept secret. The Master of Glamis is at Newcastle, you can guess for what. You will seek not for the Master, but Mr. Lion, at the direction written hereon, and the letter, as well as the safe-conduct, are on behalf of Captain Brown. You are Captain Brown for the occasion."

"I like not," said I, "to misknow my own name."

"Well, it is a thing we must all do in these times if we would live. You must take things as you find them. You will do it to save your own life and the lives of your friends, and for any other things you may have an eye to in this country; for, if all tales be true, there are such things for you, Andrew Eviot."

"I understand you not; but you have made me sure on the other side of the Border. Have you thought of how I am to reach the Border from this side?"

"Well," he said, with some hesitation, "we all have to run some risk. I reckoned that you might travel without notice as far as Leith; the passages are not watched for you. On Leith sands a party of my Lord of Bothwell's men will await you; they have been, so far, on business of their own, but you had best not ask them what it was. You can ride with them as far as you please, or leave them when they are clear of the Lothians. The rest of the way is easy enough."

"But what is the purpose of all this?"

"Now, mark me, my Captain. Our native Prince is on the point of concluding a League with the Queen of England, which will give him a sum of money in annual rent which would turn the head of any Scot in this sweet kingdom of ours. If this be done while my Lord of Arran sits at the stern and steers the ship there is an end of you and me, for there will be no further quarrel between him and the Queen of England. Of course this must not be. Our only hope is to have the banished Lords set loose—we can make no head here without them—and to gain

that we must shuffle the cards. The old woman
has brought those poor devils to poverty and
misery because they took her advice ; for her I
go in daily dread of six inches of cold steel; and,
in sooth, she has left the whole of us to the mercy
of the devil.

"Well, we have no choice but to force her
hand. The Wardens of the Middle March will
hold a day of truce on the 26th of this month,
and — 'tis no hard matter — there will be then
such a scene as will flutter Hampton Court. The
old she-devil who rules the roost there is a woman of a proud stomach, and she will not easily
forgive it. I will take care that it is laid at my
Lord of Arran's door—fear not for that. It will
be for you to see that the thing is done—always
under the style and title of Captain Brown."

"But I must have some more definite instructions than these."

"The Master of Glamis will tell you all you
desire to know. I have told you enough to carry you to Mr. Lion, at Newcastle. Now, Andrew, lad, this is a meeting for business, and I
do not ask you to forgive my abruptness, for I
know you understand such matters. But it will
not be long before we meet under very different
circumstances."

I have never wavered in my admiration for

the extraordinary skill and genius of this man, and I can truly say that I never knew one who had so great a power over me. He was very young, but he had the craft of a man of seventy; and in his intercourse with men he had a charm which was due not solely to his youth or the grace of his manners, but to the sympathy he showed to all things human. If he fell, as he did some years after this, into one of the pitfalls laid for him, I can only say in his purgation that he partook of the frailties to which all men are subject who fly at the highest game. But to me, as I have reason to say, he was a true and constant friend, and his misfortune grieved me sorely.

After our business was concluded we walked together towards the point where he had landed, speaking of things indifferent and heedless of danger. But when we were not far from the spot I seized him by the arm and bade him lie down. About one hundred and fifty yards from the shore of the Inch were two boats, apparently at anchor; the boat which brought him had vanished. Once on the ground, and seeing this unexpected sight, I bade him follow me, and, crawling on my hands and knees, made the best of my way towards the southern side of the island. When we were sufficiently out of sight of the strange boats I rose to my feet, and, again seizing him by the wrist, drew him towards my boat. For a moment he resisted, and seemed to consider; then he relented, and we both ran at the top of our speed. To my great relief the boat was where I left it, and the men were waiting at their oars. No word was spoken, and we pushed off at once and headed for the point from which I had embarked.

I doubted not that these men were trusty, but we dared not speak freely before them. We could not with safety make use of Latin; but, although there was a risk in it, we spoke in French, for speak we must, and time was short.

"Understand you that?" said I.

"Not entirely."

"Well, you have been tracked, or, what comes to the same thing, you have been observed on your way hither, or you have a traitor among your men."

"Thank you for the last suggestion; I fear it is too true to the mark, for a man above corruption is hardly to be found." He might well say so, who knew his own history so well.

"They surprised your men," said I, "where you left them, gagged them, and rowed out some distance from shore, the better to observe. And here comes in the wisdom of your precautions, which I was inclined to scoff at. It has not oc-

curred to them that there was another boat on
this side of the Inch, and they will lie off where
they are until the light comes, in the expectation
that they will then take you without trouble."

" It is like enough," he said, ruefully.

" Well, you must come with me as far as Edinburgh, where you will be safe until you can bring
your friends together."

" Nay," he replied, " I am not so witless as
that. I cannot be absent from the Court and
my master while this League with England is in
the wind. They have played me a trick, but I
will play them a better one in return. Leave me
to go my ways when we land, and ride for your
life. I know every inch of the ground. Whatever happens, you must not be found here. The
ship waits for you at Kingorn."

And so it went. We gave our boatmen more
drink-silver than they were used to see, for a
good service deserves to be well paid, and if ever
good service was done it was this. Then he vanished into the thicket, while I started at a round
pace for Kingorn, followed by Carryg and John
Sloan.

As we hoped, I met with no difficulties. If
my departure from Strathearn were known, it
seemed that none took much notice of it. Whatever might be thought of the purpose of my

companion on St. Serf's Inch, mine at least was
unknown; and I had cause to think that even
my presence on the island had passed without
suspicion. However that might be, the passage of the water was not spied upon for me,
and it was still early morning when I landed
at Leith.

A score or so of horsemen were grouped together on the sands whom I naturally assumed
to be my Lord of Bothwell's men. But they
gave me no time for inquiry, for I had no sooner hailed their leader than he signed to me to
fall in, and started his troop at a round trot.
This man—who was one named Peter Bell, but
called by his friends and enemies Gelly Jock—
told me that his orders were to wait for the in-
coming of the Kingorn boat and no longer, and
that he knew me on the instant by the description furnished to him.

"Ye see," he said, "that time is siller to poor
lads like us fra the Border, who must live by
honest trade."

In truth the company presented a strange sight
on this ride. They took with them a large number of led horses—apparently they dealt for the
most part in horse-flesh. They had not been satisfied to come abroad with one dagger and one
brace of pistols apiece, for they literally bristled

15

with deadly weapons, some of the latest fashion, and others such as men had used in the days of Halidon Hill. From their saddle-bows hung a profusion of hacquebuts, petronels, snaphances, knives, whingers, and daggers, which men are not used to carry abroad at one time from their own dwellings. One man had a bagpipe, another had three pairs of spurs, others had various articles of domestic utility. I could scarce commit so serious a breach of courtesy as to ask whence came this merchandise; but Peter Bell looked with favor upon a jest, if only it were grim enough to take his fancy.

"Trade is brisk, sir," said I.

"Aye, it's no that bad," he replied, looking lovingly at a pair of new pistols, which he had evidently negotiated on this trip; "it never was better; but how long will it last, man? Yon's a sad question for Border lads. The exchange is a' in our favor the noo, and, as ye see, we are not sleeping away our time. But if a' tales be true, his Highness is for entering into what they ca' a League with the English. If he does that, God pity us, there will be no more trading for these braw lads. Man, there will no be a horse stolen—or, as I might mair justly say, bought or sold—on either side of the Border. The country will be ruined; but there will not be sa mony

Scotts and Elliots cheat the widdie as does the day."

I parted with this good man and patriot in Teviotdale. I think we had a regard for each other.

We travelled thence to within a mile or two of Newcastle without challenge or greeting from Scot or Englishman. The light failed before we reached the city on the evening of the second day, and our beasts were spent, so that our progress was slow, when a considerable party, coming from behind, rode past us. For the most part they noticed us not; but one, having observed us earnestly, said to his fellow:

"Who may these be? The buck's cloak hath a turn I have not seen before."

"More lousy Scots, most like," was the reply, given in a grumbling tone.

"Ha!" cried the other to me. "Who are you, sir? What is your name, and what may your business be here?"

"And who may you be?" I returned, somewhat angered. "It is not my habit to give my name to the first who hath the impertinence to ask it."

Whereupon he who had spoken slightingly of my nation raised his wand, and one cried from behind: "Fie! if I could cut the thrapple out of him." But when I had drawn my sword the other gentleman, with some appearance of good-humor, interposed.

"Come, come," he said, "I can have none of this. I had best tell you, sir, as you appear to be a stranger, that I am Lord Hunsdon, the General Warden of the Marches, and this is Sir John Forster."

"If your lordship had begun by telling me that, the questions had been answered ere this. But it is scarce kindly to allow one to ride at your elbow who insults strangers who have provoked him not, and doubtless would refuse the ordinary satisfaction due to a gentleman."

"Sir John Forster is a man of warm passions and hot words; but believe me, sir, he hath an honest heart."

"I must have liberty to doubt that. I never knew one of a generous nature to insult strangers who were guests in his country."

"And whose guest may you be?" roared the knight at me. "Who bade you come to Newcastle?"

"I carry your own Queen's safe-conduct in my doublet; and if she be satisfied to give it me, am I to account to you for what my business is?"

Whereupon the two spoke together apart, and

my Lord at length told me that I must attend
him until he was satisfied as to my safe-conduct
and my business in England. In effect I was
his prisoner, and might be detained for a month
while inquiries were being made. So I rode into
Newcastle by the New Gate with my Lord
Hunsdon's party, whereas I should have been
constrained to wait outside until the morning
but for this chance.

By the gate I noticed one going towards the
city wall whose face and figure attracted me.
His strongly marked features betrayed his na-
tionality, and although he was but soberly attired
there were several apparently in attendance on
him, and his demeanor was such as to catch a
stranger's attention. As I glanced at him I saw
that he looked at me curiously; and methought
I might not have another chance, so I cried out
loudly to him:

"Sir, I am a Scot travelling with the Queen's
safe-conduct to visit one in this city, and without
offence, warrant, or suspicion, my Lord Hunsdon
leadeth me with him a prisoner."

But when this person heard me he turned his
back and hurried away, as one who would hear
no more of such matters.

CHAPTER XIX

My Lord Hunsdon carried me with him to his lodging, where he gave me in charge to some of his servants, saying that he would speak with me in a few minutes. The treatment I had from his servants was not over civil, but I could better bear it than the bluff insolence of Sir John Forster. As the minutes went by they became weary of their charge, and, thrusting me into a small cabinet or chamber at the rear of their apartment, turned the lock upon me.

One hour went by, and then a second. I began to think I was forgotten, and to look about me with a view to passing the night in this wretched cabin, when the door was thrown open and I was bidden to come out. But this was no summons to answer for myself to the General Warden of the Marches, for the gentleman I had seen at New Gate stood within the apartment, and, advancing to me and taking me by the arm, marched me so into the street. This he did without so much as uttering one word. When we were outside he bade me hold my

peace until he told me to speak, and then he led
me back to the Gate, and so on to the city wall.
We were followed by the persons I had seen
with him before, all heavily armed, each man
carrying a brace of pistols. At last he turned
to me and said:

"I have had a hard job to convince that old
pig-headed Englishman; but it is done, sir,
though at some cost, as we shall find. But, to
do things regularly, you are here to visit—"

"Mr. Lion, at Newcastle."

"Precisely. Well, young man, your wits are
strong enough to have told you ere this that I
am Mr. Lion; but if you wish to be assured that
I am I will whisper to you one or two matters
which will satisfy you."

As I insisted upon this being done, he whispered a name and some other matters in my ear
which were more than enough for the purpose.
Then he asked for my letter of commendation,
and, after glancing at it by the light of a torch
and putting it away in his pouch, he took me
again by the arm, and began afresh our walk
upon the walls.

"I had the devil's ain shindy with yon creature Hunsdon. He's like a thrawen fiend when
the name of Scot is but mentioned. At first he
was for not seeing me, but I sent him a message

which I knew he would understand; I cannot,
however, with honor repeat it to you. He was
but ill pleased to see me, the auld sinner; and
when he learned that I sought the release of his
prisoner, he was for putting me to the door
again. For he is a mighty proud cock, and
crows ower loudly on his ain dunghill. But I
minded him that, before he turned me away, he
might as well ask my name, and he saw something in my face which made him believe that I
had given him good advice. And when I had mentioned to him a name I need not repeat here, for
even these accursed English stones have lugs, he
burst out into a great anger, asking how I dared
come there when the Queen his mistress had ordered me to remain in London, and threatening
to send me to join you down the stair.

"Well, Captain David, I took his tantrums
very quietly, with now and then a laugh which
I could not smother. And when he was done I
told him that he would have to pipe another tune
to me, else he was like to learn ere many days
were passed more about Mr. Lion than he thought.
Whereupon I clapped upon his nose some papers
which I thought would be wholesome to those
who breathe this foul Newcastle air; and when
my cock sees the signature to them the feathers
of his tail fall down and all the fight dies out of

him. But he sware maist horribly against the
Queen his mistress, as he calls her, and my Lord
Burghley, saying that the Scots are left free to
come and go as they like in this city, that they
parade the walls at midnight in great numbers
and armed to the teeth, and that even the General Warden of the Marches may not find a fault
in them. But the body kenned that I had him
by the lugs, and he had no choice but to let
you go.

"Now, sir, there's a bad side to this, and I
would not for much that it had chanced. My
Lord Hunsdon is the sworn friend of the Earl of
Arran, and ye need have no doubt that yon
horseman making to the gate carrieth across the
Border the news that I am here. The auld pock-
pudding Hunsdon would never have nosed it
out for himself; but I could not have got your
release without telling, and now he will write
and tell his mistress what a smart fellow he is.
When Captain James knows the news he will
not lose his time, and I shall have to look to my
own life here. But, God be thanked! there is
one thing he does not and cannot know. He
may not guess what Captain David Brown is
going to do on the 26th day of this month."

"Captain David," said I, "does not know himself."

"Ah! I forgot," said the Master, with a grim laugh; "that pompous old pumpkin hath so infected me that I scarce think of anything but his purple face when he saw my writings. But to business. David, man, we found none so meet as you to do this thing for us. If you fail—well, you know we are powerful for little. If you do it—I can speak for others, and those not of the least—your service will never be forgotten, either by them or the Master of Glamis. I mean by this that our gratitude will be very plainly made known to you. To be short, the Laird of Ferniherst rides on the 26th of this month to meet yonder noisy, empty-headed auld bottle, Forster. I will give you a letter written by my Lord of Mar to one Halyday, his officer on the other side of the Border, charging him to furnish you with a force which will be not less than half a hundred lances. You will take these men with you on the morning of the 26th, and you will so carry the matter that the day of truce shall be set at naught, and Sir John Forster's force driven off the ground. That will be enough for our purpose, for it will cause an earthquake with a good deal of noise at Hampton Court. The details I must leave to your discretion, for I would not hamper you with instructions, well knowing that one in Newcastle cannot direct the movements of a force at Cock-law. I would only counsel you not to expose yourself too much, as Forster and some of his people have seen you here."

"I think there will be no danger of that," said I; "but as you have touched the subject, I would say that I ride a horse which is so marked that many would recognize it with ease. More-over, it is sore spent with travel, and my men and I can hardly start on the moment without giving the cattle a rest."

"David, this is a job in which delay is impos-sible. You must pass out of the gate to-morrow morning as soon as it opens. Leave the horses to me; I will find them for you, and I will keep yours until—not for long, I trow. I have said all I have to say here, for the open air is the only place for such talk; but I will now show you something within about which we need not speak."

He thereupon took me to his lodging, where he showed me a plat or plan of the Middle March, whereon the valleys of the Bowmont and Kale water were displayed, flowing to the north from the Border, being parallel to each other and but a mile or two apart. I saw also the route the Warden of Scotland would take in approaching the place of meeting at Cocklaw, which lay, as it seemed, about the sources of the Bowmont water.

Assuredly I was weary when I lay down to rest. My mind was so excited that I would gladly have gone without sleep; but the Master took upon himself all our arrangements, which he said were his own, and even roused me in the early morning with his proper hand. Thus it came about that, before we had been twelve hours in Newcastle, and, I must own, to the satisfaction of my party, we were well started on our way back to Scotland.

The letter which I carried with me ran as follows:

"CHARLES HALYDAY,—Be it known to you that the Laird of Ferniherst, the Warden of the Middle March, will ride on the 26th day of this month from Kelso to hold a day of truce with the Warden of England at a place indifferent nigh to Cocklaw. We therefore bid you to warn our tenants within the County of Roxburgh to be in readiness to ride with him. You will also give warning to Andrew Ladely, of the Thirty Acres, to concur with you therein. This letter will come to you by the hands of Captain David Brown, under whose commands our tenants will place themselves; and we charge them through

you to obey him in all matters, being one of
skill in everything pertaining to the art of war,
as if we ourself were present. You will conceive that this movement must be kept as secret
as possible, even from the Laird of Ferniherst;
but in case any should bide from the raid, you
may assure them—always in private—that ere
many weeks are gone we will return to our own,
and we shall not be ignorant of the names of
those who are contrary to our wishes. You will
learn further in this matter from Captain David
when he is with you, and will in all things obey
his wishes.—At London, this 12th day of July
1585.   MAR.

" To CHARLES HALYDAY,
    " Our officer in the County of Roxburgh."

If my business had been in Strathearn, or Fife,
or the Lothians, I should have come stealthily
upon the worthy officer. But in the country of
the Kers I knew that I breathed a different air.
The hold of the Court over the Borders was com-
paratively slight; and where Charles Halyday
dwelt there were no furious searches after men,
for if there had been, in those days no man
sought for there would have been found.
Charles Halyday was my Lord of Mar's assured man, and no easy part had he to play

while his lord and master was in disgrace on the other side of the Border. He went over with me the list of tenants, some of whom he refused to warn, on the ground that it would be dangerous to tell them so much. But with Andrew Ladeley's men he reckoned that at least fifty horsemen would answer to the call, although their feudal superior was disgraced and banished from his country.

If they had but known the service expected of them I doubt whether a dozen of these men would have shown their faces at the rendezvous. But all the information they had was to meet beyond Hounam Kirk at six hours on the morning of the 26th of the month on the service of my Lord of Mar and the Warden, to put themselves there under the orders of Captain Brown, and to be secret. These were men of rare spirit; and once in the open were likely, as it proved, to turn back for no man.

I chose the glen beyond Hounam for the rendezvous because, having intelligence that the Warden would lie at Kelso on the night of the 25th, I knew that he would ride to the March by the Bowmont Water, and it was my part to travel by another route. So it came to pass that, at six hours on a rare summer morning in the year 1585, I found myself face to face with more than fifty horsemen, as proper a set of men as I ever saw. And great need they had to be so, for no man who could not fight for his life might live on that border.

I made them a little speech, in which I told them not much beyond that there was a suspicion of foul play, and that it was the wish of my Lord that they should be near the spot where the Wardens were to meet, but that their presence should not be disclosed to the Laird of Ferniherst unless it should become necessary. Therefore some caution must be used in approaching the spot, so as not to create an unnecessary panic.

Thereupon I drew the whole party to the left into a path which strikes over the hills towards the Bowmont Water, and when we came behind Mow Law I halted them for a space, sending two men to the top of the Law with instructions to look down the Bowmont valley. These men were placed so far on our side of the Law that, while they could see everything in the valley on the other side, the Warden's party looking their way would have seen nothing, if it were not their heads. So we had due warning of the Warden's coming.

Once we knew that the Warden had passed, on his way up the water, the point where the

Calroust joins the Bowmont, we moved forward again until we halted beneath a steep knowe on the Kelsocleuch Burn, at no great distance from the place of meeting.

At this point the March between Scotland and England runs on the line from which the water falls to the north and south. Therefore two parties travelling, one from the north and one from the south, to meet each other, must gradually ascend for many miles, and then are scarce like to see each other until they meet. At first I left my men in the Kelsocleuch glen, mounting myself the shoulder of the hill to see what was going forward; but by degrees I advanced them until they were only hid from the Warden's party by the round of the hill.

The Laird of Ferniherst was first upon the ground, and had with him close upon four hundred men, a number somewhat exceeding the usual force; but the Warden on the opposite side was Sir John Forster, whom no Scottish Warden would meet without certain precautions. There was also, as there always was, a large gathering of the rascals of Teviotdale, some openly crowding upon the Warden's force, and others lurking in little corners to see what prey might by accident come their way. To this Sir John Forster I had no liking, and though I had more serious reasons for being where I was, I was also glad to be there for his sake. He passed for a bluff, honest soldier. He may have been brave enough; and as for soldiering, he was good for hard knocks; but of the military art, as it was understood in Europe, he knew nothing. As for his honesty, we Scots who know the figure he cut in the affair of the Reidswire and this matter of Cocklaw can say two words to that.

It was not long after the Wardens met and had begun to call their bills when a little disturbance was begun. An English horse-boy was caught in the act of stealing a pair of Scottish spurs, which I have little doubt had been skilfully exposed for the purpose of tempting him. The rascals on both sides ran together, and I thought my moment had come. I had divided my men into three companies, each stationed to the side, and a little to the rear, of each other; and I only awaited a certain signal, but it came not then. The Wardens ran out of their tent, and Sir John Forster offering to deliver the culprit to be hanged, if need be, the tumult died away, and the Wardens went back to fyle a bill upon Gyles Douglas, of Berop.

But the fire was still smouldering, and ere many minutes one by the Wardens' tent, whom

16

I had been watching, held up his hand. Whereupon, before any one well knew what was happening, my horse were thundering through the
Wardens' camp. Forster's men did not wait for
us, but scattered like chaff, south, east, and west.
As we passed the Wardens' tent the Laird of
Ferniherst ran out with his drawn sword, and
would have cut down the man who rode nearest
to him, but that Forster seized him round the
waist, and would not part with him, because, as
I heard afterwards, he feared that his whole train
would have been put to the sword if the Scots
Warden had left them.

It happened that in the press the Lord Rus-
sell, the eldest son of the Earl of Bedford, was
shot—whether by accident, or of purpose, or by
whom, none can say. But he had no more right
to be upon the ground than I had, and he had
wandered apart from the Wardens' tent with
some of his own people when he met his death.
It was no part of my design to shed blood if it
could be avoided; and although we pushed the
pursuit for four miles into English ground, no
other life was lost on either side.

As may be supposed, we were careful not to
return by the way we came. When I had rallied
my men I took them over the March by the head
of Coquetdale without any sort of hinderance,

and without the loss of a single life. Most of them were alive to the necessity for secrecy on this raid, and I had little difficulty in restraining them from the ordinary amenities of the Border; but in some the taint of sin was too strong to be wholly suppressed, and there were a few sheep and goats, with a bullock or two, in our ranks when I disbanded them by Oxnam Water.

I had done my part of the work. And as one —he was an Englishman — was pleased to say afterwards of this enterprise, it could not have happened better. It was for others to do the rest, and they did it so well that the Queen of England pressed for the delivery of my Lord of Arran, and the King my master cast him into the Castle of St. Andrews. And though this man was sent after a few days to vegetate at Kinneil, and in the end broke forth and regained the King's presence, his credit with the English Queen was finally destroyed.

CHAPTER XX

I now found that Captain David Brown was in a somewhat narrow shift. It was scarce likely that any would know him for Andrew Eviot; but if David Brown were taken in Scotland he would be delivered out of hand to my Lord Hunsdon, and if he were taken in England he would be hanged without ceremony. So on neither side of the Border could he well be comfortable.

On the whole, I judged it best to retire, until matters were more advanced, into the Earl of Bothwell's country; and there an asylum was cheerfully offered to me without too much curiosity as to my reasons for seeking it. It was enough for my Lord that I preferred the air of Liddesdale for the present. From beyond the Hermitage I wrote to Mr. Lion, at Newcastle, and to my accomplice of St. Serf's Inch, telling them where David Brown might be found, and entreating them to remember him when more serious work was in hand. I had no need to speak to them of the Wardens' meeting at Cocklaw, for men talked of nothing else for a month. Thereafter I fell into a low, monotonous life, wandering daily about the Nine-Stane Rig; for time drifted, and I began to fear that nothing would come of the Cocklaw Raid.

On the 6th of August the King rode out of St. Andrews for Stirling. It was said that the Plague of Pestilence had grown apace, so that it carried off no less than four thousand persons, and that the Court became alarmed at the increased mortality. But I know not whether such was the true reason, for the house of Kinneil, where my Lord of Arran was ordered to reside, is at no great distance from Stirling. Moreover, my Lord had fitted out and kept in readiness on the Western Sea certain ships for some particular of his own. Many designs were put to these ships; but there were some who said that they were meant to carry my Lord and his Highness, if need be, to the coast of France. Sure it is that letters passed every day between my Lord and the King, and my Lady made frequent visits to Stirling Castle.

Then came news that the Queen would give the exiled Lords permission to go abroad—to Germany, it was said; though when she did, as was well understood, they headed straight for the Border. Whereupon my Lord of Arran broke his ward, and came openly to the Court; and there ensued some space of time during which there were such conspiracies and intrigues as no Christian Court hath seen the like, either before or since. For my Lord of Arran, had he been able, would have slain the Master of Gray even in the King's closet, and there were many who would have slain my Lord out of hand, but that they had no chance. For neither of these men could lessen the favor of the other with his Highness, and both were so closely guarded by their friends that a man with a free sword could not find his occasion. But Mr. Edward Wotton, the English ambassador, trembled at his own shadow, and at last, so greatly did he fear it, that he mounted a horse and rode in haste to Berwick, leaving his baggage and the whole of his train behind him.

And there were many other motions and enterprises. For certain blundering hot-heads had a purpose to kidnap the King; but it was some carrion bird and not the eagle they took in their toils. Then there came to my Lord of Arran sundry boxes of bullion from that fury of hell, the Duc de Guise, and it was reported that his Highness would entertain the Antichrist. And this was said with some show of reason; but well I knew that the Prince, though he might allow others to put it forth by way of policy, had no thought of such apostasy. These and many other designs ran through the Court at Stirling, until men with the coldest heads knew not where they stood. But the Queen of England as yet moved not.

The time seemed long to me, who lived not in the heat of these intrigues, and who dared not to go near them. But early one morning there came a horseman up the brae to the house in which I dwelt; and the horse was very weary, from which I gathered that his rider had travelled through the night. Such a sight was an event there, and I went forward to meet the stranger, when, to my astonishment, my eyes fell upon my old dragon Barabbas.

"Well, old trickster," cried I, "you are generally an ill wind to me. What do you bring me this journey?"

"Even a letter, Captain."

"Ah! your fingers have an itch for letters," I replied, taking the packet he brought forth from his pouch and breaking it open.

It was from my Lochleven friend, and told me not much that I did not know. He was grateful for what I had done, but had not time to write further upon that. He had a very anxious time, but nothing he had gone through could equal what was before him. The banished Lords would cross the Border within three days and meet at Kelso, whither he bade me go and seek out the Master of Glamis, who would assuredly have need of me. But until the crisis came he himself was constrained to tarry with the Court in the midst of an army which, outwardly at least, was hostile to his friends. And this he wrote from the Castle of Stirling.

When I had read the letter I raised my eyes and saw Barabbas looking at me with a strange expression.

" I suppose, sirrah," said I, " you know all that this letter contains."

" I suppose I do, Captain."

" Well," I continued, seeing a sort of grin on his ugly mouth, and noticing again the strange expression of his eyes, " have you any message to give me by word of mouth ?"

" There is no message."

" Then why stand you gaping at me ? Speak out, man ; what is it ?"

" I was thinking, sir, I had better have spoken to ye when we last met."

" Better, indeed, my man ; for if my name is Andrew Eviot you will have to answer for a good deal before many days be past."

"For the love of Christ, dinna speak to me
that gate, Captain."

"You'll hear worse, I promise you, before all
is said and done."

"Speak not so, I beseech you. I will hide
nothing from ye, and I have somewhat to tell,
if only—"

"If what, you rascal? Think you I will make
a bargain with you?"

"Nay, sir; but hear what I have to say, and
then judge. I couldna have spoken before without betraying a confidence which even a servant of Captain James would hold sacred. I
confess I had more ado with your affairs than
ye will like to hear; but it moveth me that
ye will pardon what I did when ye ken what
I did it for. Before ye came to Ruthven Castle there was a lady keepit therein with some
closeness—an unfortunate lady, but yet gracious.
And because she was unfortunate, and gracious
even to Rusty Rynian, to whom no man was
wont to speak without a curse, I pitied her.
With my ain hand I had ta'en her father's
horse by the bridle at the back of Benbuck,
and I carried him, I and those that were with
me, to the Fastcastle. By some means she has
since found some part of the truth of this;
but I dared not tell her, for the band of my

service forbade that I should so betray my master."

"A quaint philosophy, and worthy of Barabbas ; but go on."

" By many small services I won her to believe me to be her faithful servant, and such indeed I have been. One night, some time after ye came, I was brought to her presence by a signal, which I need not stay to describe, but which I weel understood. The secret passage ye saw the last time ye were at the castle took me to the parapet without the knowledge of any but this lady. I found her in great trouble, for she had but just learnit that the King had promised my master, the Earl of Arran, that he should have the gift of her marriage so soon as he had recovered a certain chain and jewel which he had lost. It marvelled me that the news should so upset her, for surely it were better for a lass to be well married than mewed up in Ruthven Castle."

" Go on, sir ; it is not given to you to know the things which even the ancient Solomon could not understand."

" My marvel was even greater when I heard that she had given the chain and jewel to you, believing that you would deliver it to his Highness the following morning, but knowing not that she had sealed her own fate. So great was her distress that I bethought me of an expedient, which I own was very hazardous; but to her I said nothing beyond this, that if she would lend me the chain of calcedonies about her neck I would serve her to some purpose. In the end I got the chain, but before I came so far I was fain to promise that not a hair of your head should suffer through what I was in purpose to do.

"Now ye may guess in part what I did. I knew my Lord had written two letters—one to be carried by you, sir, to the King, the other to be delivered by Joshua Henderson to the Laird of Kilsyth. But I knew also the habit of my Lord; and having taken a squint at the letter to the Laird of Kilsyth, I altered the direction, and placed it in your breast at the same moment when I took from ye the other letter."

"You are an accursed thief!"

"But I did waur nor that. To change the letters was nothing; there is no a ryper in the country who can touch me for nimbleness and softness of finger. But what I did further I could scarce have done had ye not fallen into a very deep and sound sleep. For I drew the gold chain with the X Jewel from your craig and put the calcedonies in its place."

"You scoundrel! Know you not that you disobliged his Highness, while you robbed me of the credit I might have won, and put me to some shame in the presence of my Prince?"

"In truth, I ken it, sir; but I also ken that I saved my young lady from a marriage which filled her with disgust."

"Aye," said I—I had not thought of that—"so you did, man; so you did. And—I will not say you did wrong. There, I call back my hard words to you. But you have more to tell me. I will hear you out. Where is she?"

"I may tell ye now without harm that she escapit from the castle on the night of the fire to the house of one of her father's tenants. It was for my part in that that I was scourgit at Stirling, but I would bear much mair nor that for her. If she had keepit close none would have known, but she was possessed with the thought that her father was at the Fastcastle, and when she began to inquire about it Captain James and his spouse got knowledge of where she was, and carried her off to Kinneil. But I have waur still to tell; for Captain·James, either because he is angered at the lady's spirit, or that he hopes to get news of the King's jewel from her, has carried her with him to Stirling; and folk have said that he will take her with him to France in the ship which awaiteth him on the western coast. It was this news that made me beg leave to carry the letter to ye; for I believe not indeed, Captain Eviot, that ye will desert the poor lass in this strait."

"No, no; that indeed I will not. But you have not finished your tale, man; for one thing you have forgotten to tell me. Where is the jewel?"

The man looked embarrassed, and cast his eyes on the ground; but he answered me:

"As I told ye before, the jewel is in sure keeping; and I promise ye that when Captain James is safe I will deliver it to ye, and to no one else. More than that I canna say."

I knew this man to be as obstinate as a mule, and I was in the mind to take his promise; for though his philosophy of service was all his own, there was one person to whom, as it seemed, he had been a faithful servant.

"I will take your word," said I, "for what it is worth, and your body as security for it; for as I ride to-morrow morning you shall ride with me, and part not with me until the delivery is complete. But I warn you that there is one who will not take your conditions as kindly as I have."

"So be it, sir; I canna mend it. The lass shall get no harm through any faintness of heart in me."

So we rode on the following morning to Kelso, where a great company was met to welcome the banished Lords; and, as all know, we marched from thence to Falkirk without hinderance. A force of five hundred picked horsemen was appointed to look to it in especial that neither his Highness nor my Lord of Arran should make his escape; and having my own purposes in view, I prevailed that I might be joined with this force. From Falkirk we made a rapid descent upon Kinneil, but found that my Lady had gone towards Edinburgh; and, as Barabbas had told me, Jean Uchiltrie had been carried to Stirling by my Lord.

By the evening of the 2d of November we came, being now grown to a great army, to St. Ninian's Chapel, which is but a mile from Stirling. And all that night my Lord of Arran watched upon the walls, for he feared those that were within more than all the host without. But when the day came we entered the town by a close above the West Port; and though the Colonel offered a sharp resistance for a space, the Earl of Arran's men, having little stomach for the work, retired into the castle. The town being in this way free of the contrary party, and our soldiers occupied in securing their positions, there was great reiving of horses and goods by Will Kinmonth's bairns, who regarded neither friend nor foe in this pursuit of their trade. And I have since heard that my old friend Peter Bell was behind nobody in the zeal with which this free commerce was prosecuted.

The place was thus practically gained, for those within the castle were divided, the Master of Gray, Sir John Maitland, and the Lord Justice-Clerk being in effect of our own party. Moreover, had it been otherwise, its reduction was only a matter of days. But the castle being, as one expressed it, "rammed full in a manner of great personages," our leaders were not willing to let any of them escape.

It chanced that it was known to several who were with us that there was a secret postern on the western wing of the castle; and care having been taken to block this exit, a strong force was posted hard by it, in which by good-fortune my company was included. For there were still fears that Arran might abscond, and take with him the King, because the ships still lay on the West Sea which should have carried them to France.

Having heavily barricaded this postern with brushwood and branches of trees, the main body of our company retired a little space, leaving a small number for immediate guard upon the spot. After we had lain there some two hours or more there came a sort of movement on the inside of the postern, and I crept up close, the better to listen. I heard the irons put into the lock, and the plain sound as of one trying to push the gate open. As that succeeded not, there followed some whispering, the intent of which reached not my ears. Then I heard a low, measured voice which I could not mistake say:

"A bonny posture this for a crowned and anointed King!"

I ventured thereupon to say, in a voice to be heard of him who had spoken:

"Was that his Majesty who spoke?"

"That it was," was the reply, "whoever ye may be. And a sad place we are in for a born Prince. Who may ye be, man? What do they ca' ye?"

"Even Andrew Eviot, sir, your own loyal subject, whom ye may not have forgotten."

"We forget no loyal subject, sir. But what kind of loyalty ca' ye this? Canna ye open the yett, man? I charge ye, Andrew, upon your loyalty, open the yett."

"I cannot do it, sir," I said; and I added, with a certain amount of hypocrisy, "I would do it fast enough if I could; but it would give me an hour's hard work to clear away the barricade, and long before that I should have a dozen swords inside me."

"Then who is in command here? Bid him speak with us without delay."

"The Master of Glamis commands us." I was in error here, as I discovered afterwards; but it was a lucky mistake, for the reply it produced was:

"God save us! Then there is no help, for yon is a hard-handed man, as we know to our cost. But I looked not to find you here, Captain Andrew, to bar our path."

"I am not here for any such purpose, sir, but to render you a token," and I clambered over the brushwood and presented at the eye-hole through which his Majesty had been delivering himself the topaz which he had given me some months before.

"What's yon? God's banes! what is it? Aye, I see it now. And it's the blithest sign we've seen for many a long week. It almost reconciles us to— And where is yon, Captain Andrew, that ye wot of, for I take it by this sign that it is in safe hands."

"I have the surest information that it is in safe keeping, but I cannot obtain possession of it from those who have it until my Lord of Arran is in hand." Here I put the matter some-

17

what too stiff, but I had an eye to my own object.

"What!" cried the King, evidently indignant, "would they be making conditions with their lawful Prince?"

"Nay, sir," said I, smiling to myself as I thought of the conditions his own nobles would make with him within a few hours; "they made conditions with me which they would not venture to offer to your Majesty."

Here, for the only occasion in my experience, the King lost his cue, for, excited by the nature of his position and the prospect of recovering his jewel, he cried out:

"But they'll never have him in hand. He's gone man—clean gone!"

"Gone?" said I, amazed.

"Aye, gone by the North Yett over the Brig."

Never did subject run from his native Prince as I ran from that postern. As my arms were long, so were my legs, and as my wind was good I ran fast, holding my sword by the scabbard.

When I came in sight of the river the light was beginning to fail; but my eyes were good, and I could see some horses under a clump of trees on the far side. That gave me hope that I was not too late. As I came nearer I made out four horses, one man, and what appeared to be two women. I was now descending the bank to the river when a boat shot out from the river-side. There was one man in it, who rowed himself across. When he was half-way over he paused to throw something into the stream, and when he landed on the other side he made the boat fast to the stump of a tree and threw the oars into the river. There was no mistaking the tall, powerful frame of Captain James.

While I took all this in I had noticed that the stream was somewhat swollen by the autumn rains and the current strong. So I altered my course and struck the water some seventy yards above the point from which the boat put off. I lost no time in throwing off my armor, and, discarding my pistols, committed myself to the stream.

It chanced that I took the water at the moment when the fugitive was engaged in tying up the boat, so that he saw me not. But it seems that I was seen by Joshua Henderson, who stood by the horses under the trees, for he ran hurriedly down to the edge of the stream and pointed to me. Then both men drew their pistols, and presently I heard the bullets cut the water near me; but the distance was too great for a sure aim, and they seemed to wait for my landing, walking down the bank to meet me as I came ashore.

Then for the first time I began to think I had been too foolhardy; but it was no time to think, and I put the thought from me.

While they were firing at me I swam with my head up-stream, and, as I still wore my steel bonnet, kept my face averted from the opposite shore, hoping in that way to escape a bullet through the brain. Now for a brief space I turned my head again, and I saw what the two men who watched me could not see. A figure stole out from the gloom of the trees, loosened the boat from the stump which held it, sprang into it, and with one push sent it out into the stream. By this time I was more than half-way across, and the current was bearing me with fatal precision to the spot where stood my Lord of Arran and his man. When I saw the boat drifting towards me, and could no longer mistake the woman who had set it loose, I had a different mind. Timing the speed of the current as well as I might, I swam so as to catch the boat as it passed me; but I might have missed it after all my endeavors but that a hand which I well knew came forth to save me. With infinite difficulty, and no small danger of swamping the boat — for my dress was heavy and full of water, and my arms sadly in the way —I clambered over the gunwale. But as I cleared the edge of it I felt a sharp sting on the back of the neck, and I sank down into the bottom of the boat.

There was a strange sound. It said "gurgle, gurgle, gurgle." It came at intervals; it went on for a long time—a very long time. Would it never stop? It wearied me.

Then there was a "lap, lap, lapping," which came with the gurgling sound; and finally the gurgling ceased, and there was nothing but "lap, lap, lap"—at first very faint. And I was glad, for the gurgling sound pained me.

Then the lapping grew louder, and I liked it not so well. And it grew still louder, and inflicted such torture upon me as I have no words to express. By degrees it became louder and louder, until methought the sound had destroyed the sense of hearing. And, as it seemed to me, I awoke as from a hideous dream. But it was dark. I tried to speak, and my voice sounded as a whisper. But I did say, for I heard the words:

"Where am I?"

And a voice, which seemed to come from long

ago, and had been with me night and day for many months, said:

"Upon the sea,
Alone with me."

THE END

By A. Conan Doyle

By GEORGE DU MAURIER

TRILBY. A Novel. Illustrated by the Author. Post 8vo, Cloth, Ornamental, $1 75; Three-quarter Calf, $3 50; Three-quarter Crushed Levant, $4 50.

Certainly, if it were not for its predecessor, we should assign to "Trilby" a place in fiction absolutely companionless. . . . It is one of the most unconventional and charming of novels.—*Saturday Review*, London.

It is a charming story told with exquisite grace and tenderness.—*N. Y. Tribune.*

Mr. Du Maurier has written his tale with such originality, unconventionality, and eloquence, such rollicking humor and tender pathos, and delightful play of every lively fancy, all running so briskly in exquisite English and with such vivid dramatic picturing, that it is only comparable . . . to the freshness and beauty of a spring morning at the end of a dragging winter. . . . It is a thoroughly unique story.—*N. Y. Sun.*

PETER IBBETSON. With an Introduction by his Cousin, Lady * * * * * ("Madge Plunket"). Edited and Illustrated by GEORGE DU MAURIER. Post 8vo, Cloth, Ornamental, $1 50.

That it is one of the most remarkable books that have appeared for a long time is, however, indisputable.—*N. Y. Tribune.*

There are no suggestions of mediocrity. The pathos is true, the irony delicate, the satire severe when its subject is unworthy, the comedy sparkling, and the tragedy, as we have said, inevitable. One or two more such books, and the fame of the artist would be dim beside that of the novelist.—*N. Y. Evening Post.*

PUBLISHED BY HARPER & BROTHERS, NEW YORK.

☞ *The above works are for sale by all booksellers, or will be sent by the publishers, postage prepaid, to any part of the United States, Canada, or Mexico, on receipt of the price.*

R. D. BLACKMORE'S NOVELS.

PERLYCROSS. A Novel. 12mo, Cloth, Ornamental, $1 75.

Told with delicate and delightful art. Its pictures of rural English scenes and characters will woo and solace the reader. ... It is charming company in charming surroundings. Its pathos, its humor, and its array of natural incidents are all satisfying. One must feel thankful for so finished and exquisite a story. ... Not often do we find a more impressive piece of work.—*N. Y. Sun.*

SPRINGHAVEN. Illustrated. 12mo, Cloth, $1 50 ; 4to, Paper, 25 cents.

LORNA DOONE. Illustrated. 12mo, Cloth, $1 00 ; 8vo, Paper, 40 cents.

KIT AND KITTY. 12mo, Cloth, $1 25 ; Paper, 35 cents

CHRISTOWELL. 4to, Paper, 20 cents.

CRADOCK NOWELL. 8vo, Paper, 60 cents.

EREMA ; or, My Father's Sin. 8vo, Paper, 50 cents.

MARY ANERLEY. 16mo, Cloth, $1 00 ; 4to, Paper, 15 cents.

TOMMY UPMORE. 16mo, Cloth, 50 cents; Paper, 35 cts.; 4to, Paper, 20 cents.

His tales, all of them, are pre-eminently meritorious. They are remarkable for their careful elaboration, the conscientious finish of their workmanship, their affluence of striking dramatic and narrative incident, their close observation and general interpretation of nature, their profusion of picturesque description, and their quiet and sustained humor. —*Christian Intelligencer, N. Y.*

PUBLISHED BY HARPER & BROTHERS, NEW YORK.

☞ *The above works are for sale by all booksellers, or will be sent by the publishers, postage prepaid, to any part of the United States, Canada, or Mexico, on receipt of the price.*

By MARY E. WILKINS.

PEMBROKE. A Novel. Illustrated. 16mo, Cloth, Ornamental, $1 50.

JANE FIELD. A Novel. Illustrated. 16mo, Cloth, Ornamental, $1 25.

YOUNG LUCRETIA, and Other Stories. Illustrated. Post 8vo, Cloth, Ornamental, $1 25.

A NEW ENGLAND NUN, and Other Stories. 16mo, Cloth, Ornamental, $1 25.

A HUMBLE ROMANCE, and Other Stories. 16mo, Cloth, Ornamental, $1 25.

GILES COREY, YEOMAN. Illustrated. 32mo, Cloth, Ornamental, 50 cents.

We have long admired Miss Wilkins as one of the most powerful, original, and profound writers of America; but we are bound to say that "Pembroke" is entitled to a higher distinction than the critics have awarded to Miss Wilkins's earlier productions. As a picture of New England life and character, as a story of such surpassing interest that he who begins is compelled to finish it, as a work of art without a fault or a deficiency, we cannot see how it could possibly be improved.—*N. Y. Sun.*

The simplicity, purity, and quaintness of these stories set them apart in a niche of distinction where they have no rivals. —*Literary World*, Boston.

Nowhere are there to be found such faithful, delicately drawn, sympathetic, tenderly humorous pictures.—*N. Y. Tribune.*

The charm of Miss Wilkins's stories is in her intimate acquaintance and comprehension of humble life, and the sweet human interest she feels and makes her readers partake of, in the simple, common, homely people she draws.—*Springfield Republican.*

PUBLISHED BY HARPER & BROTHERS, NEW YORK.

By MARIA LOUISE POOL

AGAINST HUMAN NATURE. A Novel. Post 8vo, Cloth, Ornamental, $1 25.

The contrasts of Northern and Southern temperament and manners . . . are brought out with a fidelity that reveals intelligent acquaintance and trained powers of observation. This novel is far above the average.—*Watchman*, Boston.

OUT OF STEP. A Novel. Post 8vo, Cloth, Ornamental, $1 25.

An exceedingly interesting story, with elements of both tragedy and comedy wonderfully involved.—*Philadelphia Telegraph*.

THE TWO SALOMES. A Novel. Post 8vo, Cloth, Ornamental, $1 25.

The character conceptions of the story are all good and well wrought out, the situations are all logical and expressive, and the interest in the problem keeps fresh.—*Providence Journal*.

KATHARINE NORTH. A Novel. Post 8vo, Cloth, Ornamental, $1 25.

From an artistic and literary standpoint, Miss Pool's best work. . . . The story is an intensely interesting one, and is most skilfully constructed.—*Boston Traveller*.

MRS. KEATS BRADFORD. A Novel. Post 8vo, Cloth, Ornamental, $1 25.

Miss Pool's novels have the characteristic qualities of American life. . . . The author is on her own ground, instinct with American feeling and purpose.—*N. Y. Tribune*.

ROWENY IN BOSTON. A Novel. Post 8vo, Cloth, Ornamental, $1 25.

A very delicately drawn story in all particulars. . . . It is excellent art and rare entertainment.—*N. Y. Sun*.

DALLY. A Novel. Post 8vo, Cloth, Ornamental, $1 25 ; Paper, 50 cents.

There is not a lay figure in the book; all are flesh-and-blood creations.—*Philadelphia Ledger*.

PUBLISHED BY HARPER & BROTHERS, NEW YORK.

☞ *The above works are for sale by all booksellers, or will be sent by the publishers, postage prepaid, on receipt of the price.*

By CHARLES DUDLEY WARNER

THE GOLDEN HOUSE. Illustrated by W. T. SMEDLEY. Post 8vo, Ornamental Half Leather, Uncut Edges and Gilt Top, $2 00.

It is a strong, individual, and very serious consideration of life; much more serious, much deeper in thought, than the New York novel is wont to be. It is worthy of companionship with its predecessor, "A Little Journey in the World," and keeps Mr. Warner well in the front rank of philosophic students of the tendencies of our civilization.—*Springfield Republican.*

A LITTLE JOURNEY IN THE WORLD. A Novel. Post 8vo, Half Leather, Uncut Edges and Gilt Top, $1 50; Paper, 75 cents.

THEIR PILGRIMAGE. Illustrated by C. S. REINHART. Post 8vo, Half Leather, Uncut Edges and Gilt Top, $2 00.

STUDIES IN THE SOUTH AND WEST, with Comments on Canada. Post 8vo, Half Leather, Uncut Edges and Gilt Top, $1 75.

OUR ITALY. Illustrated. 8vo, Cloth, Ornamental, Uncut Edges and Gilt Top, $2 50.

AS WE GO. With Portrait and Illustrations. 16mo, Cloth, Ornamental, $1 00. ("Harper's American Essayists.")

AS WE WERE SAYING. With Portrait and Illustrations. 16mo, Cloth, Ornamental, $1 00. ("Harper's American Essayists.")

THE WORK OF WASHINGTON IRVING. With Portraits. 32mo, Cloth, Ornamental, 50 cents.

PUBLISHED BY HARPER & BROTHERS, NEW YORK.

☞ *The above works are for sale by all booksellers, or will be sent by the publishers by mail, postage prepaid, to any part of the United States, Canada, or Mexico, on receipt of the price.*

www.ingramcontent.com/pod-product-compliance
Lightning Source LLC
Chambersburg PA
CBHW030636030726
47497CB00006B/1814